*Death Stalks
the Cheyenne Trail*

Also by William E. Vance
DRIFTER'S GOLD

Death Stalks the Cheyenne Trail

WILLIAM E. VANCE

DOUBLEDAY & COMPANY, INC.

GARDEN CITY, NEW YORK

1980

Library of Congress Cataloging in Publication Data

Vance, William E
    Death stalks the Cheyenne Trail.

    I. Title.
PZ4.V222De [PS3572.A425]   813'.54
        ISBN: 0-385-15518-2
Library of Congress Catalog Card Number: 80-926
Copyright © 1980 by William E. Vance
        All Rights Reserved
Printed in the United States of America
        First Edition

Copy 1

*Death Stalks
the Cheyenne Trail*

CHAPTER ONE

The two pistols flashed fire and angry thunder at almost the same instant.

Almost.

A stiff March wind, blowing across the pistol range at Fort Myer, Virginia, ruffled the waters of the Potomac, whisked away the smoke quickly. The smell of gunpowder, acrid, pungent, remained behind.

Watching the smoke disappear, Dave Coppers emptied his .44 Colt and reloaded with cartridges he took from his brown corduroy jacket pocket.

Seventy-five feet away, he watched his opponent do the same thing while two permanent party soldiers looked on at this strange and unusual contest that took place at least once, and at times even twice or three times, each week.

He'd drawn and fired with a relaxed ease that gave him an edge in most of his weekly duels on the pistol range with Harlan Gage, a fellow Secret Service agent in Washington, D.C., and a lifelong friend.

Gage walked toward him accompanied by a soldier bearing a silhouette target—the top part of a man's body. The target Gage had fired at stood beside Coppers with a neat .38 Special bullet hole one inch to the right of the heart.

"According to my split second hand, Mr. Coppers fired first." The soldier wore a faded field jacket with the brighter outlines of a corporal's stripes in the color, indicating this man had once been a noncommissioned officer.

"It's a draw," Coppers said.

"Don't ever give anything away," Gage said and handed Coppers two silver dollars. "You win—as usual."

Coppers passed the two silver dollars to one of the soldiers. "Why don't you fellas have a beer on us?"

"Thanky, Mr. Coppers, sir," the ex-corporal said, his face brightening. "Thanks a lot."

The two soldiers watched the men mount the horses at the shack near the edge of the range and ride away, side by side. The younger soldier said, "That big ugly one, who's he?"

"Mr. Coppers? He was guarding McKinley when he was kilt by that crazy anarchist sonofabitch."

"The hell you say! What he do now?"

"Still works for the Secret Service, I hear; but they made him a clerk or janitor 'er somethin' after McKinley died."

"Keerist! That's tough."

"He's shore a bona fide hero, though. With the Rough Riders in Cuba. Got the Medal of Honor. You know somethin'? When he comes out here he could get a twenty-one-gun salute if'n he wanted it. He rates like a general 'count o' that Medal."

"What the hell did he do to get the Medal of Honor?"

"Don't know exactly. Maybe saving Roosevelt's life . . . or maybe it was just gettin' the colonel's horses aboard the *Yucatan* —or maybe it was capturin' the *Yucatan* and holding it for the Rough Riders. I hear tell he had to lick half the New York infantry outfit so's the colonel would have a ship to get to Cuba on."

"Keerist! Fighting to get into a war!"

"Well, it was the on'y war we had goin' then, feller."

"Well, well, well, what the hell you know about that?"

"We'd better get our asses movin'. Here comes the sergeant."

Coppers and Gage rode their horses side by side, walking them past Kraftburger's Dairy Farm and across the bridge with the lions' heads, the Washington monument looming in the distance. Coppers' black hair curled from under his Stetson; the hat and rider's boots somehow did not clash with the brown corduroy suits he affected, the belted jacket loose around his wide, thick shoulders. His was a rugged face, with high cheekbones, a gift from his Cheyenne mother; though his even features were scarred, a gift from the Spanish at San Juan Hill, he was a singularly attractive man. The matrons and politicians' daughters in the nation's capital found Coppers charismatic and appealing —and hard to get to know.

"Something is up, Dave," Gage said as they came down the broad street. "Effington is on something big, seems to me."

Coppers merely nodded.

Gage looked at him perplexedly. He was a freckled, thin and wiry man with blazing red hair. Harlan Gage and Coppers had been together since their youth when Frank Gage took young Coppers in after his parents had been killed by revenge-seeking outlaws. "Ever since Effington broke up that Spanish spy ring in Canada he's been a cloak-and-dagger nut."

"He got to become chief of the Secret Service through that little roundup," Coppers said.

"Yeah, yeah. I keep thinking—"

"You're gonna hurt your brain," Coppers said.

"Effington is killing you off. Not with a bullet. That'd be more merciful. He's doing it with—"

"Let's drop it," Coppers interrupted, speaking quietly but forcefully.

Gage sighed and shrugged.

They rode their horses down Pennsylvania Avenue, keeping to the gutter to avoid wheeled traffic, including the noisy, smoky gas buggies. When they reached the Treasury Building they dismounted and Gage took the reins of Coppers' roan gelding. "I'll put 'em away," he said.

A matched pair of white horses hitched to the President's surrey stamped impatiently in the driveway of the White House across the street, and Gage tilted his head in that direction.

"The colonel is going somewhere. It'd be easy to get to him, Dave."

Coppers grinned. "I'll do nothing of the sort, Harlan. And think for a minute—what would Effington say if he got a memo from Roosevelt instructing him to restore me to field duty?"

"He'd do it," Gage said.

"See you later," Coppers said and entered the building, climbing the dim, musty stairway to the third floor. He made his way through a clutter of desks to reach his own. He took off his coat and hung it by the window to rid it of the smell of gunpowder.

He went to his desk, unshucked the shoulder holster, and dropped it into the bottom drawer and slammed it shut.

It was just a little less than five years ago, he reflected, when he'd traveled to Buffalo with President McKinley and the presidential party, to attend the Pan-American Exposition. Three men to guard the President: David Coppers, Harlan Gage, and Dan Thomas. Dan was now chief of the President's bodyguard. The year, 1901, and the Secret Service had only recently assumed responsibility for the White House Guard. Coppers smiled without knowing it, remembering his pride in his new assignment. Quite a jump for a roughshod Wyoming cowboy, which he'd been before the Rough Riders, and Cuba.

Coppers remembered it all as vividly as though it happened the day before, with regret and agony. The morning of September 5, 1901, the presidential party set out for Niagara Falls. Coppers rode in the President's carriage with Mrs. McKinley between Coppers and the President, who appeared to be in good spirits. The President read over the speech he planned to make at the Exposition that afternoon. Gage was in the carriage behind, with the Secretaries of War and Treasury. The President's personal secretary, a man named Cortelyou, was livid with rage at being in the third carriage. Buffalo's mounted police provided escort for this excursion, riding ahead of and behind the caravan.

Coppers was fascinated with the falls. He knew the falls were familiar to the President, but McKinley seemed to enjoy the view and the awesome roar of the falling water as much as Dave.

After a basket lunch in one of the many parks in the area, the procession headed back toward Buffalo and the Exposition.

Coppers remained close to the President while McKinley gave his speech outside the Hall of Music. The speech was mercifully short. Mrs. McKinley went away to the Hall of Dance, accompanied by Gage, at the President's request. Coppers and Thomas followed the President through a side door into the great cavernous Hall of Music and onto the dais that had been erected at one end of the huge building. The room was crowded with men, women, and children who wildly applauded McKinley. Despite his vacillation and indecision, McKinley was growing on the American people.

With his arms folded and within reach of the President, Coppers watched the portly man as he shook hands with the people filing by him. He patted a little golden-haired girl on the head, smiled and half-turned to the next man in line, a medium-sized man wearing dark and shoddy clothing. The man's right hand was covered with a bandage. The President extended his hand to the man. The President's hand was roughly pushed aside and smoke erupted from the bandaged hand as two shots rang out. The President staggered back as Coppers leaped on the assassin, bearing him to the floor, wrenching the gun from his bandaged hand.

Pandemonium broke loose. Men shouted, women screamed, and children cried fearfully as the enormous crowd surged back and forth in mounting hysteria.

Soldiers who'd been on the edge of the dais came to Coppers' aid, beating and pounding the slight man who made no struggle at all.

The President, clutching his chest with both hands, said weakly, "Let no one hurt him."

Coppers waved away the angry soldiers and jerked the man to his feet, hustling him along the edge of the dais to turn him over to security guards and police at the door. The crowd turned ugly and threatening, and cries of "Lynch him!" rang out through the building. Coppers hurried back to the President as a line of police, military, and Expo guards began pushing the crowd toward the exits. Fainting women impeded the exits, and hysterical children cried aloud for their parents.

Covered with sweat, Coppers was dimly aware of all this as he asked the President to lie down on the stage to await the arrival of medical help. He had no idea as to the extent of the President's wounds. An awful sense of guilt was rising steadily inside him. He asked himself why he'd not been more alert, more wary of the crowd.

The fact that the Secret Service had only recently assumed responsibility for the President's safety, and it was a job new to all three of them, did nothing to relieve his self-reproach.

After McKinley's death, Chief Effington relegated Dave to a dead-end desk job, little more than a clerk, reading reports from the field, initialing inconsequential memoranda that played no important role in the Agency's operations, which included investigation of counterfeiting, providing protection services and investigative potential to other government departments, and occasionally furnishing bodyguards for distinguished foreign visitors. Coppers got none of those details. Effington made sure of that, eagerly assisted by Buford Skiles, Effington's shadow.

The deeper the regret, Coppers thought, the harder it is to put words to it. He shuffled the papers on his desk restlessly, got up and walked to the window, and stood looking out at the spring colors and the groundkeepers digging around flowering shrubs. The presidential team and handsome carriage had long since departed the White House driveway.

Coppers steeled himself and returned to his desk, pulling toward him the stack of papers. A Denver operative was reporting again the appearance of unsigned bank notes taken in a holdup of an express car in 1896. Only there was now a difference. The bills appearing in Denver were skillfully executed forgeries.

Coppers shrugged and passed on to the next report and then pushed it aside while he rolled a cigarette. Something Gage had said nagged at him. Effington was up to something "big." Coppers moved his big shoulders again restlessly.

I'm always restless, he told himself, after shooting at the pistol range. He'd told himself that before and even entertained vague notions of quitting it. But he knew he would not. He lived for those days on the pistol range, not only the shooting but the ride across the river which invariably brought back memories of his early days on the Rafter G, which was the only home that made sense to him, and that too was long gone. Coppers had thought often of resigning and going back to Wyoming, but he resisted the urge, feeling somehow that it would be an admission of defeat. He didn't harbor these thoughts often, of life as it might be on the Rafter G, or some other ranch, perhaps his own. He'd kept up with the ranching business through the *Stockman's Journal,* and he knew things were changing radically from the time he and Gage had deserted the ownerless Rafter G to rendezvous with the Wild Bunch at Steamboat Springs, to enlist, en masse, in the Rough Riders. That too had come to nothing.

There were a number of brown cigarette-paper ends in the ashtray when Coppers finished the field reports. He was starting

on the current Memos of Instruction & Information when Buford
Skiles, Effington's assistant, approached his desk.

Skiles, a tall, thin man with prematurely white hair, had har-
bored a grudge against Coppers when Coppers bested him in
competing for a place on the White House Guard. Skiles had
started in the service as a clerk and by hard work and politicking
had worked his way up to become number-two man in the department. That achievement had never cooled his desire to be an
agent in the field. He felt he needed the experience if he ever ex-
pected to succeed Effington.

"Chief wants to see you," Skiles said without greeting.

"Me?"

"Yes."

"What's it about?"

Skiles made no effort to hide his dislike of Coppers. "He'll tell
you that when he sees you. He's waiting." He wheeled and went
back toward the Chief's office.

Coppers got his brown coat and slipped into it, vaguely dis-
turbed. This was the first time the Chief had sent for him since
Coppers had been severely reprimanded for dereliction of duty.
He felt pain even thinking about it.

The Chief didn't look up as Coppers entered. He held a match
to a long black cigar, and he slowly waved it out and carefully
placed it in an artillery shell used as an ashtray. He was a slight
man with cold blue eyes, thin lips, thin black hair, and he wore
wire-rimmed glasses.

"Have a good shoot today?"

"Yes, thank you." Coppers wasn't aware that the Chief knew
of his twice weekly visits to the Army pistol range.

"Ever think of joining the pistol team and competing?"

"No, sir."

Effington scowled. "Just as well." He opened a folder and
looked at it intently while the silence built. Still looking at the
folder, Effington said, "You're originally from Wyoming?"

"Yes, sir."

Effington put the cigar in his mouth and puffed determinedly.
He took the cigar out of his mouth and waved it at Coppers.
"There's work to be done out there."

"In Wyoming?"

"Yes, Wyoming. What's so unusual about that?"

"Perhaps you know something I don't," Coppers said mildly. The Chief lifted his eyes from the folder and looked at Coppers, clearing his throat. There was a twitch to his thin lips that might have been a smile.

"A million dollars in unsigned treasury notes was taken from a Union Pacific train at South Pass in 1896," he said. "The money was being returned to the engraving department here to correct an oversight—add the signatures of the Treasurer of the United States and the Secretary of Treasury. When the train robbers found out they had incomplete bills, they sat on their haul. But they've found an engraver or someone to forge the signatures, and the money has been turning up in Denver, Salt Lake City, and"—he consulted the folder again, adding—"and San Francisco."

"I've only read the report from Denver," Coppers said. "Sounds like a widespread operation. Based in Wyoming?"

The Chief nodded, his cold eyes chillier than ever. "We suspect that Butch Cassidy and Big Nose George pulled off the job."

"Butch has been in South America for the past four or five years," Coppers said.

Effington gave a derisive snort. "That's what he'd like everybody to believe."

"I believe—"

"It's immaterial," Effington said curtly. "The information we have—by the way, Coppers, we don't believe Cassidy is involved in the appearance of the forged bank notes. I—oh, what the hell, man. I'm not going to sit here explaining—"

"It's not necessary."

"Of course. As I was saying, we've reason to believe one of our own Treasury experts on forgery, who resigned two years ago for reasons of health—he had consumption—is living on a ranch in Wyoming. This man is also an engraver. He could very well do it and do it very well."

Coppers nodded noncommittally.

Effington smiled dryly. "You were a cowboy once upon a time. Think you could become one again?"

Coppers felt a sliver of hope build inside him. His brown face was passive, giving no evidence of his racing thoughts. "I think so, sir," he said in a steady voice.

"They're in favor now. Cowboys, I mean. We've one in the White House."

"From what I know, a very good one. Started from the bottom."

Coppers saw the cold eyes get chillier, but he was determined not to let his admiration for Colonel Roosevelt's achievements be put down by the older man. "He turned out to be the greatest war hero since U. S. Grant," he said, reasonably. "He seems to know what he's doing. He's the youngest President we've ever had—"

"The President is not the subject of our discussion."

Coppers moved his big shoulders. "You brought it up," he said, and added, "sir."

Effington nodded. "Yes, I did. But we must get on with what I called you in for. A lot of our agents dashing around in the sagebrush, or whatever, might upset the applecart. If you believe you can do it—bring it off—you can drift in as a—an itinerant whatever. . . ."

"It's called riding the grubline. An unemployed cowhand is called a saddle tramp by some." His inflection said he didn't like the term.

Effington closed the folder and shoved it away from him with a frown. "We don't have enough information, Coppers. You'll have to dig it out yourself. Gage will go ahead of you and make necessary arrangements. But listen to this: he'll return here and you'll be on your own. That's all, Coppers."

Coppers rose from his chair. "Thank you, sir," he said.

"Don't thank me," Effington said with a thin smile. "I've my doubts about you, Coppers. Your success—or failure—will prove or disprove my feelings in the matter."

Coppers smiled crookedly at Effington, wheeled and walked to the door, and let himself out, reflecting that the last interview with Effington had been much different than this session.

Only a handful of people were left in the musty old building when Coppers strolled down the stairs and out into the spring balminess of Washington. He stopped at Mamma Pelote's and had a beer and a bag of nuts. With half his mind preoccupied with Effington's orders, he hardly noticed when Gage sat at the marble-topped table opposite him.

"How'd it go?"

Coppers shrugged. "I got a job out in the field."

"Good. So have I. I've been briefed and here's what Skiles told me Effington wants: You're to look as much like a down-and-out line rider as you possibly can. I'm to go ahead and line up whatever you might need. Your jump-off point is Cheyenne."

"Cheyenne?" Coppers sipped his beer.

Gage nodded, grinning. "You won't believe this, Dave. You're gonna wind up on the ol' Rafter G. Surprised?"

Coppers nodded. "I'm ready to believe anything, Harlan. After today. Surprised? No, I'm way past that."

Gage leaned across the table. "The old man is edgy as hell, Skiles tells me. Wants me to leave on the next train."

"Is he setting me up, Harlan?"

Gage jerked erect. "Hell fire, Dave! What're you asking me—"

"Whoa up there, buddy," Coppers said. "Effington hates my guts. He'd use government authority and funds to make a dummy out of me. Set me up for firing."

"What makes you think that?"

Coppers shook his head. "No proof. Just a feeling in my gut." He met Gage's eyes. "Why the Rafter G, our old home place?"

"Well, this fella Boynton, used to work for the Treasury, bought the old place for taxes. It's now the Slash B. Effington has got some information from somewhere that Boynton is capable of forging those signatures."

"It's—the ranch that is—closer to Laramie than Cheyenne. Is Effington trying to make things harder for me?"

Gage shook his head. "No-o-o, I asked him about that, Dave. He said Cheyenne would be better because you might be recognized in Laramie."

Dave chuckled, fingering his battered nose. "Who?"

"I don't know." Gage rose, stretching. "I've got a train to catch," he said. "I'll have everything ready when you get to Cheyenne. I'll contact you there." He walked out of the tavern without a backward look.

CHAPTER TWO

Coppers was home in twenty minutes. He let himself into the old gingerbread-fringed home operated as a boarding house for "Refined Ladies and Gentlemen" by Ida Mae Courtney. The parlor was empty at this time of day and he passed through it to his own room.

He stood before his small shelf of books and selected *Goodman on Forgery* and walked to a rocking chair by the window and turned on the gaslight. Mrs. Courtney had acquired the new electricity but the light flickered and was unreliable; Coppers seldom used it.

He leafed through the book until he found the passage he had looked for and read it to refresh his memory as to what constituted forgery. It confirmed his memory that a person could commit a forgery yet be innocent of criminal action—if forced to sign by another.

He read Goodman's fascinating book on forgery for half an hour and then rolled a cigarette and smoked it, gazing out the window as he thought about the trip west. He was becoming restless, impatient to be on with it, and he recognized the signs with wry amusement at himself.

A tap on the door ended his rumination and, before he could rise, the door opened and Ida Mae entered the room, changing it noticeably. She came quickly to his side and put her hand on his shoulder, her beautiful face troubled.

A rather tall woman of thirty-two, her dark flamboyant beauty was scarcely marred by the rigors of running a boarding house inhabited mostly by minor government officials.

Coppers looked up into her dark eyes with their shadowy black lashes, thinking for the thousandth time how beautiful she appeared to him.

He got to his feet. "I'm going back to Wyoming," he said abruptly and watched consternation spread across her attractive face.

"Oh, no," she said. "I can't bear the thought, Dave."

He placed his hands on her shoulders and pulled her to him. "I'll miss you," he said.

"You're quitting the Secret Service?"

"No. I can't talk about what I'm going to do."

"I understand." She closed her eyes and then opened them wide. "Oh, Dave, Jack is going to miss you so." Jack was her twelve-year-old son.

"I want Jack to have Roanie, my horse. Do you mind?"

He felt her stiffen. "You're going to do something dangerous, I know!"

He laughed. "I might get run over by a team of those galloping fire-engine horses or, worse yet, one of the newfangled gas buggies."

"You're going— Why? Why?"

He touched her cheek. "I don't want—I can't talk about it, Ida Mae. But I'll tell you this: it means a lot to me."

She slipped away from his hands. "I—I'm going to my room, Dave, because I feel like I want to cry and I don't want you to see me." She turned and fled from the room.

Coppers was cleaning his pistol, the one he'd used on the Army pistol range that afternoon, when Jack came in without knocking, his dark face sullen, pouting.

"Ma said you're going away." He stared at Coppers and it seemed that some emotion, perhaps hate, was reflected in his dark eyes, eyes so like those of his mother.

Coppers nodded, ramming the cleaning rod through the barrel of the .44 Colt. "Did she tell you about the horse?"

"I don't want your damn horse!"

Coppers laid the pistol aside and looked at Jack and said gently, "Ol' Roanie wouldn't like to be taken by a stranger."

A tear oozed from the boy's eye and rolled down his cheek. "Why don't you marry my ma? Why don't you want me to be your son like I almost am? . . ." He opened his mouth in silent anguish, whirled and hurtled from the room.

Coppers felt a heaviness in his chest. In that instant he saw himself at twelve years of age.

The Coppers family settled in Laramie when Dave was eight years old. Cal Coppers, his father, became a peace officer in Laramie, moving his Cheyenne wife, Ekaname, and his eight-year-old son into a small frame house painted white and trimmed with green. The town was in an uproar when the Coppers family arrived; the principal peace officer, who also ran a saloon, had been hanged by a group of irate citizens, and Calvin Coppers was hired to bring stability to the lawkeeping forces.

By the time Dave was eleven years old, he was as sinewy and quick as his Indian forebears on his mother's side. He became an excellent rider, and with his sharp eyes was able to light a match at twenty-five feet with his .22 rifle. Calvin, quietly proud, claimed that in addition to being a sharpshooter, his kid "could ride anything with four legs and hair."

Dave's straight black hair and his eyes a startling blue in his dark face made him a familiar sight around Laramie, which had become a law-abiding town under Cal's watchful eyes.

Dave's Indian friend, John Buttner, a Cheyenne, wore white man's clothing and was night watchman in the railroad yards. John's cabin nested in a crook of a creek about three miles from town and became a second home to Dave. John taught him much about the land and wildlife, how to make a bow, and what wood to use for the straightest arrows. Moreover, Dave could shoot with amazing accuracy. He learned to stalk game and to trap beaver and mink.

There was one fly in the ointment. The town kids followed after John Buttner on his evening walks to the railroad yards. The boys shouted insults and threw stones at the impassive giant who ignored them with lofty pride and dignity. Dave got into many a fistfight with the town kids who pestered John Buttner. Dave didn't win all of them.

This minor struggle continued until a traveling circus came to town one spring. The circus tents were set up in open space outside town and created a stir in Laramie, as the citizens looked forward to the infrequent entertainment.

A band of Northern Cheyenne was in one of the acts, and John Buttner, visiting the Cheyenne, talked to them in their own

language, which was his mother tongue. Buttner's image immediately changed in the eyes of Laramie residents and, more important to Dave, in the eyes of the town small fry. It struck him
as strange that merely speaking to circus Indians in his native
tongue caused this turnabout.

It was in this aura of happiness over Buttner's elevation to
town hero that tragedy struck. Returning home from school one
sunny afternoon, Dave was met by wide-eyed, breathless school-
mates, telling him his father and mother were dead, murdered
by outlaws.

Unable to believe it, Dave threw his books to the ground and
ran for home, his terror and panic mounting with each stride.

He pushed his way through the crowd in front of his home
only to be grabbed by a tall, redheaded man with an equally
flaming beard and who had beside him a small redheaded boy.

"Don't go in there, kid," the redbeard ordered roughly. He
reached again for Dave who evaded him, ducking away and running up the steps, his eyes watery and his heart beating like a
tom-tom. Dave scurried around Town Constable Al Hunter and
plunged through the door.

"Hey there boy, you can't go in there!" Hunter shouted.

Inside, Dave lunged across the parlor and halted abruptly in
the doorway of the kitchen. His father lay on the floor before the
kitchen range, the back of his head blown away by a shotgun
blast at close range. His gunbelt and pistol hung from a peg beside the outside door.

Slowly, Dave's eyes went past his father to the screened back
door. There were flecks of red and gray on the screen. His
mother lay slumped in the doorway. The tomatoes which she
had held in her apron lay scattered on the floor.

Dave's shock retreated and he started to scream only to be
choked off by the bile which rose in his throat. He gagged, puk-
ing, until his insides and throat ached. He smeared a hand across
his face, wiping away the tears and sourness.

Turning blindly, he staggered back into the parlor, bumping
into the legs of the redheaded man. He clutched the legs and
began to cry. He felt a rough hand on his shoulder and gradually
his sobs subsided, leaving his body wracked and weary.

"I'm Frank Gage," the redheaded man said. "I knowed yore

paw a long time ago. I got him to come up here, and them two devils he put in jail down in Kansas hunted him down soon as they got out. I reckon it's up to me to take keer o' you. I got a boy name Harlan, about yore age. . . ."

That is how David Coppers went to live on the Rafter G with Frank Gage and his son, Harlan.

Dave and Harlan grew up together and were closer than most brothers. Like brothers they fought one another. And the battles seemed to bring them closer together.

The last scrap happened when Dave and Harlan worked during haying time, forking hay from a wagon into the barn loft. It was the second month after Frank Gage brought Dave to live at the Rafter G. Dave had never, never worked so hard in his life, from dawn to dusk.

Suddenly, out of nowhere, Harlan asked: "Your ma was a squaw, warn't she?"

The two of them were stripped to the waist on an unseasonably hot day. Sweat glistened on their bodies, Dave's a dark brown, Harlan a dead white which never seemed to tan.

Dave's heart gave a lurch. He remained silent.

"Pa said she was a Cheyenne squaw," Harlan said.

"The daughter of a Cheyenne chief," Dave said, leaning on his pitchfork, fighting his rising anger. "You ain't got no ma," he added. "What happint to her?"

"She died when I was four. I don't remember her much."

"What'd she die of?"

"I don't know. Like I said, I don't remember much."

"Your old man probably worked her to death," Dave said.

Harlan dropped his pitchfork and leaped toward Dave, his fists flailing. "Don't you go talkin' 'bout my pa like that!" he raged.

Dave easily avoided Harlan's rush through the hay. He threw his pitchfork away and leaped to the ground. Harlan jumped after him, landing on Dave's shoulders and sending him staggering.

Dave regained his footing and backed up a step or two. Harlan came at him again, taking wild swings at him. Dave coolly punched him hard, in the stomach, and Harlan bent over, his face white, gagging.

"I don't want t' hurt you," Dave said.

Harlan straightened, the white receding from his face, leaving a ring of white around his mouth. He came at Dave snarling incoherently. Dave hit him twice, in the mouth and on the jaw.

Harlan's face screwed up, twisting, and his eyes clamped shut. He turned and put his arms on the wagon wheel and laid his head against his arms.

Frank Gage rode around the barn on his calico pony and pulled up short, jumping to the ground. "You two been at it ag'in?" he bawled. "I'll have no more of it. Git along together. You're all each othern has; you'll learn, better now than later."

His sudden rage subsided and his face became gentle and understanding as he looked at first one and then the other. Shaking his head, he remounted and rode on to the rambling ramshackle old ranch house that had been turned into a pigsty since the death of Frank Gage's wife from typhoid fever.

"I'm sorry," Harlan said, wiping his bare arm across his face. "I shouldn' a said what I did."

"I shouldn' a said what I did," Dave answered.

Silently, they went back to work, forking the hay up into the opening in the gable giving access to the hayloft.

Frank Gage ran a good spread with the help of the two boys. He'd take on extra hands in the spring, and at the beef roundup in the fall. He wasn't an excessively generous man nor stingy to a fault, being in between, and convinced that every dollar paid out would eventually lead to his ruin.

The work was hard and monotonous, with little time for anything resembling play. Frank Gage didn't believe in too much idle time on a man's hands. The two of them, Dave Coppers and Harlan Gage, turned into men early, without quite knowing when it happened.

The Rafter G prospered despite drought, rustlers, homesteaders, and sheepmen. Gage fought them all with equal abandon and it seemed that he was winning. Then came the big dryup of 1886. The range dried out, grass withered and died, and creeks, water holes, and wells went dry. The cattle weakened, grew gaunt, and bellowed ceaselessly.

Frank Gage went broke building fence, hauling water, and buying hay. He kept hoping for a break when winter set in.

When cold weather did come, it delivered the final blow, finishing him off, the worst winter within the memory of the oldest living person in the territory. Blizzards raged days on end. The land was filled with blowing snow that turned to sleet and ice. Temperatures dropped below zero and what with the high winds it was impossible to get outdoors. The three of them remained weatherbound for weeks on end, so long that time lost all meaning. All three of them went slightly mad.

When the weather broke and they were able to ride the range once more, they found the cattle, weakened by summer drought, had died by the hundreds in this latest disaster. Frank Gage was a broken man, unable to mount more than a feeble protest when a Colorado sheepman named Will Talbot brought thousands of woollies onto Rafter G range. Gage rode out to confront Talbot and never returned.

Dave and Harlan spent a month searching for Frank Gage and finally gave up. Both of them were convinced that Frank Gage had been killed and his body buried in some lonely unmarked grave.

Dave and Harlan became wandering herders working on ranches in Wyoming, Colorado, and Utah. Late in 1897, with rumors of war in Cuba in the air, they heard that a bunch of outlaws was gathering at Steamboat Springs to enlist in Roosevelt's Rough Riders. The two of them rode out, headed for that town, thinking it might be easier to get in the Rough Riders if they joined up with a gang of real tough nuts.

Ida Mae Courtney did not cry after she left Dave Coppers. She stopped by her son's room and told him that Dave was going away. The boy, big-eyed, listened to her with his mouth slack, openly disbelieving her words. He slammed down his book and ran past her, heading directly toward Dave's room, which is what she hoped he would do.

She reached her room feeling numb. She rubbed her hand across her lips, she tucked in the edges of her hair and pushed away the desolate feeling of defeat that replaced the numbness. It had been in her plans to marry Dave Coppers after she discovered he was the kind of man she could trust. Except for the facial disfigurement he'd suffered in the Spanish-American War, he was an extremely handsome man. Even the scars lent a certain attractiveness, as did the broken nose. More important to her, he was honest, direct, and he had a gentleness in him that she was unaccustomed to finding in any man selected at random in whatever level of society.

She'd had trouble enough with the other kind. Sam Courtney, her first husband, had been such a man, overbearing, untrustworthy, sly, scheming, and, in the end, very foolish.

Sam Courtney had met his death while robbing a rich old farmer in Maryland, reputed to have a secret hoard of gold buried on his farm.

Losing a husband in that manner damaged her in ways she didn't like to think about. She'd put her trust and faith in Sam Courtney as a youthful and impetuous young woman and, with his death, a small son to support, she was decidedly unfit to face life alone.

She did as well as she could. She'd trained as a midwife and moved to Washington, D.C., where she wasn't known. In the years following she'd presided at the birth of babies of the famous and near famous in the nation's capital. She won powerful friends over the years. A beautiful and vivacious woman, she'd earned enough money to purchase the very old home of a politician, who'd deserted Washington after an election defeat, and set it up as a boarding home. She had servants, a fine carriage, and many luxuries that she could easily afford. But she felt keenly the need of a man. Not just any man would do. They had filed by her, one by one, until Dave Coppers came on the scene.

She'd come to know him well, and she let him know of her feelings in many ways. She waited patiently for him to make a move, knowing it would come sooner or later. And now—he was going away to God only knew what mission. There must be, she thought desperately, some way to stop him.

CHAPTER THREE

A week after Dave's meeting with Effington, Skiles came into the big room and jerked his head. "Want to talk to you," he said in his cold neutral voice.

Dave rose and followed Skiles to a cubbyhole of an office just off Effington's commodious one.

He jerked his head toward a chair beside his desk and Dave sat down.

Skiles shoved papers and a pad of currency to Dave. "Your transportation request," he said. "Take first-class Pullman to Omaha. Get off at Omaha and buy a ticket on the day coach to Cheyenne. Gage will meet you there with the rest of the instructions."

"Any particular reason?" Coppers asked politely.

Skiles frowned his annoyance. "Mr. Effington wants it that way."

Dave shrugged. "Whatever the Chief says."

"This is a big operation, Coppers," Skiles said testily. "We've got to take every precaution. If there's anyone on the Pullman who might be connected with the deal, he—or she—will think you left the train at Omaha."

"She?"

"I don't rule out a woman being involved," Skiles said evenly. He waved his hands, indicating dismissal. "Any questions or problems come up, Gage'll take care of it in Cheyenne."

Dave took the transportation request and money and put both in the breast pocket of his brown coat. He looked at Skiles and said, "Thanks a lot, Mr. Skiles."

Skiles didn't answer but pulled a mound of papers toward him and began going through the stack, not looking at Coppers.

Fifteen minutes after Coppers' departure, Buford Skiles thrust aside his paperwork, rose from his desk, took his hat from the clothes tree, and settled the hat squarely on his head. He informed his male secretary that he would be out of the office for the rest of the day. He took the back stairs to the street.

A brisk twenty-minute walk brought him to his destination, the residence of H. Richard Donel, the Washington *Enterprise*'s star reporter. Skiles pounded the brass knocker and the reporter, in person, answered the door, peering suspiciously at Skiles over rimless pince-nez glasses, held to his lapel by a black ribbon. He adjusted the glasses, cleared his throat, and muttered, "This had better be important."

Skiles stared at the world-famous newsman without changing his expression. "I'm Buford Skiles," he said. "I—"

"I know who you are," Donel said brusquely. "What brings you to my door?"

Skiles betrayed no inner emotion, though he felt a rage build inside him which he stifled. He shrugged, staring down at Donel, a short man with round shoulders and the beginning of a potbelly thrusting over his trouser top and suspenders. "I'm here to do you a great favor, Mr. Donel," he said quietly.

"Why?"

"Let me say that I believe in what you're doing—educating the public on the President's true stripe."

Doubt glimmered in Donel's pale yellow-centered eyes. He opened the door wider. "Please come in," he said formally.

After Skiles was inside, Donel closed the door and strode past him with a nod of his head and a curt, "Right this way, Skiles."

Skiles followed the man down the hallway and into a cluttered study. Copies of Donel's most ambitious work, *The War As It Was*, filled one shelf completely. The book was of a war Donel had never experienced personally, a book he'd gleaned from a Union soldier's letters home. The book had made him rich and famous, enabled him to write his own ticket at the *Enterprise*, and to cover the Greco-Turkish and Spanish-American wars, the last where he developed a vitriolic and undying hatred for Theodore Roosevelt.

Donel pushed a chair into place and waited until Skiles was seated before he dropped into a large, leather chair that dwarfed his slight figure.

"All right, sir," he said, trying to be crisp. "What is it?"

"Maybe you'd prefer some background first?" Skiles asked, betraying nervousness for the first time.

"Just the bare facts. I'm a busy man." He stared at Skiles. "On second thought, perhaps I shouldn't listen at all. You're a public servant, a bureaucrat, and as such shouldn't even entertain ideas of policy matters and the like."

Damn pipsqueak, Skiles thought venomously, not revealing the real emotion, anger, and rage aroused by this self-important little man.

"I believe, truly believe, in your efforts to show President Roosevelt as he really is. I'd like to help you pursue this line of your investigation."

Donel licked his lips and muttered something that sounded like "Humph!" but he waved his hands for Skiles to continue.

Impertinent ass, Skiles thought; no wonder Roosevelt put him at the tail end of the column fighting its way up San Juan Hill. Aloud, he said, "There's a most important story to come to light in the next month or so, but it'll happen in Wyoming."

"Well, I went to Turkey and Greece to cover a war and the next year after that I sailed for Cuba to cover another war. With my reputation, Mr. Skiles, I can go anywhere in the world my fancy dictates."

"Yes, I know," Skiles said humbly. "That's why I'm here."

Satisfied for the time being, Donel relaxed in his chair so that his slight figure seemed even smaller. "Get on with it," he ordered.

Skiles winced but spoke with confidence. "I'm unable to give you *all* the details," he said in a solemn voice, "but I can assure you it will startle the nation when revealed. Imagine, if you will, a future President of these United States of America actively recruiting killers, outlaws, the very dregs of humanity in the West, to fill the ranks of his so-called Rough Riders." He sniffed.

"I can imagine," Donel said dryly.

"When this story breaks—if you're there to break it—the true identity of a famous outlaw will be revealed to the world—"

"Please don't write the story for me," Donel commanded.

"I could never do that," Skiles said fervently. "After all, there's only one H. Richard Donel."

"Quite. And who's this famous outlaw?"

"Butch Cassidy," Skiles said impressively. "He—"

"Is in South America," Donel said.

"No! He's in Wyoming at this very moment—well, maybe he hasn't reached there yet, but he will shortly. In due course he'll be arrested for a number of federal offenses and brought to trial —unless he resists arrest."

"You've my attention," Donel said, no longer relaxed but leaning forward now, his finger tips drumming at the armrest of his chair. "Go on."

"That's all there is to it at this moment," Skiles said. "If you leave immediately for Wyoming, take up residence at a dude ranch called the Box MB, you'll be on the scene when the story breaks."

"You've not given me enough information to make a decision," Donel said thoughtfully, though he had already made up his mind to travel west. The interest of his readers had flagged. President Roosevelt was becoming more popular all the time with the mass of stupid voters.

"I'm afraid I can't give you more at this time," Skiles said coldly, rising to bring the interview to an end.

Donel looked at him calculatingly. "I suppose I can quote you—"

"No, you cannot," Skiles said, with steel in his voice. His piercing gaze brought a faint flush to Donel's pallid features.

"Of course, of course," Donel said carelessly. "I recognize your need to be invisible." He chuckled. "I do need a vacation, Mr. Skiles, and I think I'll be going out to the Great Wild West. Thank you for bringing this to my attention."

Skiles turned away to hide his revulsion. "I can find my way out," he said.

"Of course you can, Mr. Skiles," Donel said, a chuckle in his voice. "A great Secret Service operative like you! Of course you can."

CHAPTER FOUR

Four days after his short meeting with Buford Skiles, Coppers' train arrived in Chicago. He followed the crowd out of the station to the long line of hacks waiting to transport passengers across town to a different railroad, the Union Pacific.

Among the passengers was a tired, pale woman with two small children hanging to her skirt, which was badly wrinkled.

Coppers helped her with her luggage, rode in the same hack with her, holding the small boy, and carried her luggage to the Pullman. He got her settled and selected for himself a seat as near the smoker as possible. The UP train was not as fancy as the one he'd ridden from Washington to Chicago.

The conductor, a portly man, dignified and proper, stood at the far end of the car, surveying his passengers with a probing glance, cataloguing from long experience: drummers, pleasure-seekers, and a cowman here and there. Dave Coppers watched him and made his own estimate. Somewhere in the distance the engine whistle sounded and a bell set up a clang-clang. The conductor turned and made his way out of the Pullman.

Coppers heard him call, "All Aboard!" and then call out the names of the stations along the way. Dave settled back into his seat, relaxing and trying not to think too much about the future as the train gathered speed.

He straightened as a hand touched his shoulder. The tired, pale-faced woman leaned over him. "I—I must take Katie to the dressing room," she said in an almost inaudible voice. "Will you watch Tommie—I mean, if he wakes up?"

Coppers glanced at the boy, lying on the seat, his eyes closed, his thumb in his mouth. He nodded. "Sure. Be glad to."

A man with a star on his vest behind his thigh-length black coat sauntered down the aisle. He paused beside Dave's seat and

Coppers could smell the odor of whiskey. The man went on and then turned and came back and sat beside Coppers.

"Hi, fella, I'm Shug Kruger, from up north o' Cheyenne, deputy sheriff." He offered his hand.

Coppers reluctantly accepted the hand. He had no desire to engage anyone in conversation, preferring to maintain a low profile.

"Name's Coppers," he said, slurring the name so that it came out something else. He needn't have bothered. Kruger was past noticing such things.

"Just came up to Chicago to pick up a bank robber and killer," he said, in a bragging manner. "Feller tried to make a break for it 'tween jail and the train station. I hadda shoot 'im."

Coppers stared straight ahead as the train rocked along.

Kruger went on, "Damn if'n the county ain't too cheap to pay fur first-class accommodations. I hadda make it up outta m' own pocket. I mean the difference 'tween day coach and this here Pullman palace." He looked at Coppers and saw nothing in the brown, scarred face. "Wuth it, I reckon."

The lady with the little girl returned to her seat. She thanked Coppers for watching the little boy.

"He hasn't moved," Coppers said.

"Why, Sal," Kruger boomed. "Fancy meetin' you here!" He leered at the woman who colored visibly as she moved Tommie's feet and seated herself, holding the little girl on her lap. She kept her head lowered and didn't look up. The little girl snuggled against her mother's breast and fell asleep.

"She usta be in one 'a them houses in Cheyenne, till ol' Mel Bennion took her out and married her," Kruger said with a sly grin and in a loud, penetrating whisper.

Coppers saw the woman's head drop even lower. A thin thread of anger began forming in Coppers. "I need all of this seat. Plenty seats up ahead and I'd appreciate you finding one."

Kruger rose, scowling. "Reckon I kin take a hint," he said, and went swaggering down the aisle.

The woman gave him a brief, grateful look.

Coppers dozed, listening to the sounds of the train—the clack of wheels on the rail joints and the rush of their motion, the occasional wail of the whistle's lonely cry in the night. Coal smoke, invisible but odorous, invaded the car. He felt restless and out of sorts, knowing he had to rid himself of his tiredness before switching to the day coach. The day coaches were crowded, dirty, and carried would-be farmers, homesteaders, and people looking for a new start in the promised land.

He came erect from a doze, suddenly, and looked around. The little girl, Katie, was asleep in the backward riding seat. Across from her the small boy still sucked his thumb in his sleep. The woman, Sal, was gone, apparently to the dressing room.

Coppers stood up as he heard a soft voice of protest. He looked ahead. Kruger wasn't in sight. Sighing, Coppers stepped into the aisle and went toward the rear of the car. Kruger had the woman pinned between his arms, his palms resting flat on the wall of the Pullman car. The swaying lantern lighting the car moved their shadows back and forth.

"I wouldn't do that," Coppers said, pulling one of Kruger's arms down and wheeling him away from the woman.

"Well, you're not me," Kruger said. "So just shuck off, friend."

Coppers took one step and swung. Kruger's jaw felt slack and soft beneath his fist. Kruger went back against the wall of the Pullman and slid to a sitting position. He pushed away from the wall, reaching for the pistol on his thigh. Coppers kicked his hand away and his boot went into the man's jaw and he slumped over with a groaning gasp and was still.

Coppers turned but the woman was gone. He looked down at Kruger and turned and returned to his seat. The woman was looking out the window.

"Mrs. Bennion," Coppers said.

She turned her head and looked at him.

"He won't bother you again."

"Thank you," she said. "Thank you very much. Mel—my husband was worried about something like this. He said I wasn't to look at or speak to strangers. But Shug Kruger is not a stranger." She ended her speech abruptly, her face coloring. There was a smudge of dark on her left cheek.

"I wouldn't even mention it to him," Coppers said.

She gave him a grateful smile. "Thank you. You're right, I do believe. Mel—my husband that is—has so much on his mind these days. I didn't want to leave him. But my mother passed away and I just had to go back."

"I'm sorry," he said mechanically.

"She was so old. She didn't suffer, was sick for just a little while. She lived a good and full life."

That seemed to call for a response but Coppers couldn't think of a proper one. He was silent.

She wouldn't allow him to withdraw. "Mel's a rancher. But there's no money in cows, not any more. Mel is in the middle of changing our spread into a dude ranch."

Coppers lifted his eyebrows.

She hastily added: "We're not getting out of cattle entirely. The dude ranch part is to supplement the other. We had a big group last fall, for the hunting. They were from Europe and all over, one of them a prince. We did so well, Mel decided to make it a regular part of the business."

Coppers nodded and said politely, "I wish you lots of luck."

"We'll need it," she said, sighing.

It was six o'clock when Dave Coppers stepped off the westbound Flyer in Cheyenne. He went to the end of the platform and put his bag on the planks, watching the activity attending the arrival of the train, the bustling movement.

Standing in the shadows he watched a stage drive up beside the platform, the horses under the expert hand of a humpbacked cowboy wearing a big black hat. A tall man got out and put a hand on the platform and vaulted up. Sal Bennion, the kids holding on to her, came to meet her husband.

"Whatta y' think of it?" Bennion hollered, motioning to the stage. "This here is what we'll haul our pilgrims out to the ranch in."

The tall rancher scooped up his two kids and jumped to the ground, the boy squealing, and put them on the stage. He turned and held up his arms to Sal and she leaned forward, and he put her in the stage without stepping on the ground. He shouted, "Let's get outta here, Humpy!" and vanished inside the stage which lumbered away.

Coppers had a sudden feeling of loneliness. That feeling wasn't new. He stood there, listening to the sounds of talk and laughter coming from those starting to travel and those ending it.

The engine groaned, the whistle sounded, the bell clanged, and the train moved away into the night. Coppers was damn glad to be off the day coach. He drew in a deep breath and looked at the sky. The stars were brighter here than in the east. He hungered for a look at the country in full daylight. The mountains west loomed above, seeming near yet far away.

The people were moving away now as the westbound disappeared in the folds of the hills. A man came up between the platform and the rails and stopped, looking up at him.

"Hello, Dave."

Dave answered without looking down. "Hello, Harlan. Cheyenne's kind a picking up."

"Liveliest west of Chicago. Gettin' wilder all the time."

Yellow light from the depot and waiting room spilled out on the splintery platform. Dave turned and looked down at Gage. "I can't get used to a blazing metropolis out here in the middle of nowhere."

"Not like when we rode through on our way to Steamboat Springs," Gage said. "You won't have time to get acquainted with the bright lights, Dave. Everything's ready and waiting. The Antlers Hotel, up the street. Everything you'll need. Time you got to work, old buddy."

"Gee whiz, I thought I'd have a day to get the kinks out," Dave said good-naturedly.

"Charlie Effington wouldn't like that," Harlan said.

Dave chuckled and didn't answer.

Gage went on: "Your horse is in the barn behind the hotel. Buckskin gelding. Last stall on the right. Bridle and saddle under the hay in the manger."

"Who thought all that up?"

"The Chief has a heavy hand in all this."

"H-huh. The Chief."

"Listen, Dave. The buckskin is a pretty showy horse. You go out the Laramie Road, about eighteen to twenty miles. There's a pine tree at a branching-off road, looks like an Indian war bonnet, with the feathers—tree limbs, I mean, on one side of the trunk. Take that side road couple of miles to a log cabin. Old retired railroad detective name of Max Callum lives there. He'll give you a bay for the buckskin. He'll be your contact in gettin' messages back east if you have to do it."

"You're not staying on?"

"Nope. Chief's orders. You're on your own. I'm taking the night train east and don't see me off. Good luck, Dave." He stretched up and gave Dave a key. "Room 212. I know you're not gonna like the boots I got for you but wear 'em anyway. Code book's in the lining of the boots."

"Yeah. Thanks." The two men shook hands, and Harlan turned and faded into the shadows.

Dave waited a few minutes and then headed for the Antlers, blocks away. He walked past the old stagecoach and down Central Avenue. He reached the hotel and turned into the deserted lobby, the walls of which were lined with deer and antelope heads. The sign on the counter behind the tap bell said: Ring for Service.

Dave crossed the lobby and climbed the stairs. He found the room and unlocked the door and surveyed the room illuminated by outside light filtering through the dusty window. He stepped in, closed the door, and walked across the room. He struck a match, took off the glass chimney, and touched a flame to the wick. He adjusted the wick and replaced the chimney and the room brightened.

He picked up the lamp and crossed to the door and read the sign.

Please turn on light by touching black button. To turn light off, press white button. Please do not attempt to light the globe hanging from the cord in center of room with a match. Thank you. The Management.

Smiling, Dave pressed the black button and a dim electric light came on. He blew out the lamp and carried it back to the table. He pulled down the green shade over the window and went to the bed and sat on it. The springs protested whiningly. He bounced once, smiled to himself and got up, stripped off his clothes, and turned to the washbasin in the corner of the room. The muscles rippled under his dark skin as he washed and scrubbed. The hair covering his chest was a tight mask of black falling to his hard, flat stomach. He washed himself thoroughly and toweled.

When he was finished, he got a bag out from under the bed and opened it. Gage had used his imagination too well, he thought wryly, picking up the faded and patched Levis and holding them up for critical inspection. He tossed the pants on the bed and lifted out the rest of the clothing Gage had put in the war bag. A calico shirt, in the same state of rough wear the pants had suffered. A red-and-white bandana, a battered flat-crowned black hat, well marked with sweat and indications it had been used as both feed bag and watering trough for a horse in the not too distant past.

To hell with that, he thought, and dropped the hat on top of the pants and shirt.

The war bag next presented a pair of boots, rundown heels, a hole in the middle of the left boot. Both boots were speckled with cow manure. He dropped them on the floor, determined he'd not wear them even though they were the right size. He frowned, remembering Gage's admonition about the code book.

He put on the pants and shirt. After some debate with himself, he donned the battered boots. He had some difficulty with the hat, but finally put the hat on that Gage had selected for him. He looked at himself in the mirror. "Hi, bum," he said and then took his Colt .44 from the shoulder rig and shoved it into the holster Gage had furnished. The holster was attached to a cartridge belt, which he buckled around his waist, adjusting the gun butt so as to be easy to reach. He bent down to tie the leather thong around his right thigh. He straightened, lifting the gun from the holster and shoving it back.

It was a few minutes before nine and there was an ominous rumble of thunder as he went through the lobby and stepped outside the Antlers Hotel. He found the darkness had become even darker. Across the street from him an electric light above the swinging doors of the Red Dog Saloon flickered once and went out. The sound of a piano and a woman's thin voice came to him over the loud voices and laughter coming from the pleasure palace. He listened for a moment and then turned down the street toward the depot. Gage had expressly forbidden him to see him off, but Coppers thought he'd see his friend safely aboard from a distance.

He was fifty feet from the depot when he saw the flash of yellow flame and heard the shattering report of a gun. He broke into a trot when he saw a man fall on the splintered station platform.

He leaped up to the deck and stooped over the fallen man. His heart gave a mighty surge when he saw it was Harlan Gage. His fingers went to Harlan's wrist and he found only the receding feeble beat of a dying heart that fluttered out as he pressed his fingers desperately, as though he'd instill life that wasn't there, would never be there again.

The pound of boots brought him erect. Whoever had fired the shot that killed Harlan was gone, but out of the night a man raced toward him, holding a pistol at arm's length ahead of him. Dave caught a glimpse of two men peering from the depot window.

"Stand right there, you," the man with the gun said, and light from the depot turned the star on his vest a dull yellow. "Don't make a move or I'll blow a hole through you."

Dave half-raised his hands while his thoughts raced madly through his brain. He couldn't let this man take him in or the whole plan would collapse. Yet he couldn't bring himself to swap lead with a lawman.

"Take it easy," Dave said softly. "I'm not about to make a move—" He flung his hat into the lawman's face and at the same time leaped to the ground from the platform; bending low he ran hard, away from the lights of the depot. He heard one shot when he landed, and another when he was fifty feet away. He heard no sound of a passing bullet but crazily reflected that you don't hear bullets unless they hit something or bounce off anything that deflects them.

Once in the darkness, he straightened and changed his pounding run into a natural walk.

He continued on, not letting his eagerness to be rid of the town affect his caution. He worked his way back toward the Antlers Hotel, stopping in the shadow of a tree, watching the hotel and the barn behind it.

Satisfied there was no one in the barn, he moved toward the

large dark building. He waited in the shadows for another long silent spell and then, walking swiftly, entered the barn, standing upright. He paused there for only a moment to make certain no one was inside and then went down the wide corridor between the stalls. The buckskin was there, as were the saddle, bridle, and blanket as Gage had told him. He worked fast but unhurried, saddling the horse and leading it outside. He paused there for a moment, thinking. He was without a hat and his own, an almost new Stetson, was upstairs in room 212, along with his abandoned clothing.

A man afoot or without a hat in this country stood out like a horse in a saloon. That decided him. He tied the buckskin and went at a normal walk to the back entrance of the hotel, entering without hesitation. He reached the second floor and turned toward the room he'd occupied briefly earlier, halting abruptly in midstride when he heard a woman's laugh and the deep rumble of a male voice.

He went on then and a minute later left room 212 wearing his forty-dollar Stetson, which was a better fit than the battered hat he'd flung in the lawman's face.

CHAPTER FIVE

Coppers was clear of town, out in the open, under the stars, with a soft blowing but chill wind in his face before he allowed himself to think about Harlan Gage. When he did at last come to the point where it all had to come out, he stopped the plodding buckskin and stepped to the ground, ready to face up to the full meaning of the past few hours. The full impact of Gage's murder hit him then.

In the moonlight his lips stretched thin and tight. Even his eyes changed as the up to then repressed feelings surged up, filling his chest with a physical pain, his throat choking unbearably. He felt alone, standing there among the rounded foothills of the plains that rose to the distant mountains bulking against the lighter sky.

He fisted the reins and spoke to the horse and walked ahead, the animal following so close its muzzle nudged his arm. He felt an inexpressible sadness, remembering all of it, little bits and pieces of Gage and him, from the day they pulled stakes and left the Rafter G forever to become drifters, floating from first one ranch and then another, taking each day as it came. It was a rugged life of hard work, loneliness, brief spurts of violence as they fought rustlers and landgrabbers alike.

Gage was a man to ride with, a warm, honest man with a streak of loyalty, and dependable as a branding iron.

There had been the Englishman's ranch owned by a wealthy remittance man, located down on the Wyoming-Colorado border, where they lived and worked for a time. The job was good. The Englishman, Timothy Jones, let them do the work the way they knew it should be done and paid them well. They went to town once a month, on Saturday night.

Coppers remembered the time they almost became outlaws on one of those Saturday nights. . . .

Dave had pushed his way into the saloon with Harlan close behind. The place was crowded with miners and cowboys and the latest addition—oilfield roughnecks—with the gaming tables going full tilt. Men were standing around the tables, waiting their turn, and others lined up at the bar, doing heavy drinking. The place was noisy and full of smoke. It was what they were looking for.

"Looks like a yippee night," Harlan said appreciatively.

"It's a night to howl at the moon," Dave agreed.

Feeling good, they walked to the end of the bar and waited for the busy bartender. A man came in from outside, banging open the swinging doors with a crash. He roared, "Make way fer Lawton Gary!" He apparently had just come from the saloon across the street, for he wobbled as he walked to the bar, shouldering his way roughly through the drinkers. He was followed by two gun-toting buddies who seemed as hardcase as the man in the lead.

"Come on here, barkeep," Gary shouted. "Give us a full bottle and three glasses. Don't be so damn slow."

The bartender was in the act of pouring drinks for Dave and Harlan. He frowned, shrugging. The hatchet-faced man who called himself Gary took out his pistol and tapped the butt on the bar.

"I said pronto, suds slinger!"

"You better do what he says," one of Gary's buddies spoke up. "That there Lawton Gary is the man who killed Cal Coppers and a lot o' other fast shooters."

Dave left his glass untouched, stepped away from the bar, and went down the line of men, all of them staring at Lawton Gary.

Dave stopped behind Gary, looking steadily at him. Gary glanced into the mirror behind the bar and straightened as he saw Coppers standing there, watching him. His face grew alert and he turned slowly, hooking his thumbs in his gunbelt, waiting expectantly, not as drunk as he first appeared.

"If you killed Cal Coppers you must've killed his wife, too," Coppers said calmly. "What'd you do, Gary, hide out in his home and wait for him?"

"Who the hell are you?"

A dead silence fell over the saloon. Men stopped talking. They stopped drinking. Dave felt his stomach heave, resisting an impulse to shut his eyes, as the scene in the house came back to him, more vivid than ever—his father sprawled before the kitchen range, his mother in the doorway, the red and gray splotches on the screen door, the tomatoes she'd just brought in from the small garden scattered around her.

Coppers shook his head, one quick jerk. "Why, I'm Dave Coppers," he said. "You're drunk now, Gary, and I won't bother you right this minute. But sober up and do it fast because when you're able to handle a gun I'll kill you."

Gary's face went white. He looked quickly at his two partners and saw at once they'd be no help. He went for his gun, jumping sideways as he made his draw while customers scattered wildly.

Dave waited until Gary's gun cleared leather and then in a move almost no one saw, he drew and fired into Gary's body. Gary's gun went off reflexively, the bullet plowing into the sawdust-covered floor at Dave's feet.

Coppers moved his gun to Gary's two companions, but Gage already had them covered.

"We're outta this," one of them said quickly.

"Either one of you two with Gary when he killed my folks?" Dave asked.

"Hell, no! We met up with him jes' a week 'er so ago. We was all going down to Steamboat Springs, big meetin' down there. Butch Cassidy and his bunch gonna jine up with the Rough Riders and get a pardon. We wanted to git one, too."

"Let's get the hell out of here, Harlan," Dave said, and the two of them backed out of the saloon door, still holding their guns ready.

They rode out of town unmolested.

Four days later, they approached the outlaw camp, on Bear Creek, just downstream from the hot springs. The glittering leaves of the aspen on the higher slopes sent down a silvery glimmer. The outlaws, Dave quickly counted eleven of them, were camped in a cottonwood grove in a bend of the creek.

Dave immediately recognized Butch Cassidy, though he'd never met him. The man stood apart from the others, still wearing a derby hat from some city fandango. He was a man who'd stand out, even in a crowd. He had a pleasant smile under a small black moustache, his square face without guile.

"Well, men?" Cassidy said pleasantly enough, but it definitely was a question.

"We heard you was holding a meeting," Dave said.

"You wanted by the law?"

"Well, maybe the law don't know about us yet."

Cassidy laughed. "Meanin' they'll know sooner or later?" He shook his head and looked around at the group of silent men squatting beside the smoldering fire with its blackened coffee pot. "We're all on the dodge. We figure we're damn tired of running and want to get out of this trap. It ain't no fun, not anymore, with telephone and telegraph and gas buggies." Without hardly pausing, he shot a question at them: "Pinkerton's didn't send you boys in, did they?"

Both of them denied it vehemently. "Far as I know," Dave said, "I've never met a Pinkerton."

"I heard ol' Charley Siringo was taking out after me," Cassidy said pleasantly. "A man in our business can't be too careful."

"We gonna continue the meetin'?" a voice called from the clump around the campfire.

"This been goin' on day and night for nigh on to a week," said a bewhiskered outlaw who wore a double-breasted flowery vest oddly contrasting with his range gear.

"Come on in by the fire," Cassidy invited, and turned back to the business that had brought them all together.

Cassidy squatted before the fire, poured coffee into two cups, and passed them to Dave and Harlan. He waved at his companions. "We got the cream of the crop gathered here. There's Harry Longabaugh, Elza Lay, Bill Carver, Ben Kilpatrick, Harvey Logan, and even Big Nose George over there, hidin' behind them whiskers." He laughed and the others joined in.

Dave noticed the way all heads swiveled as the sound of an approaching horse came to them. One of them stood up, loosening the gun in his holster.

The newcomer, an older, weathered man riding a good-looking chestnut rode in, carrying a hat. He tossed the hat to Cassidy and said, "Butch, this is the on'y one they had in either town that'd fit y'." He dismounted stiffly and looked glancingly at Dave and Harlan. "The marshal tol' me to tell you all to be outta these parts by sundown tomorrow."

Cassidy took off his derby and tossed it in the creek and clapped on his new hat, pulling it down and then shoving it on the back of his head. "And this young feller who brought me a hat, is Jefferson Davis Stoneham, better known as Dakota for some reason or other. He's sure not from Dakota but he might have been there once."

Dakota led his horse to the creek and let it drink and then put it on a picket line and joined the group. "Word I get is that the law in Denver know what we're up to and they're waitin' for us."

"Wouldn't you know it?" Cassidy asked unsmilingly.

Squatting in the outlaw circle, Dave and Harlan sipped coffee, and listened in fascination as the outlaws debated. Now and then one of them would take off on a story of some past incident, usually related to breaking the law, to enliven the proceedings. All of them agreed on one thing: Together they could lick the Spanish Army, but they'd never be allowed to do it.

The outlaws concluded that it would be impossible for them to enlist as a body. The law was aware of their plans and would be waiting. The only way it could be done would be for them to break up and travel to distant points and sign up individually. Chances of them reuniting to fight the Spanish would be slim. None of them discussed their plans. Outlaw wise, all of them, they'd learned the hard way that, if they let out too much information about their movements, the law would eventually hear about it.

When the meeting was about to break up, a woman named Lil drove her buggy into the clearing and greeted the outlaws, some of them by name. She looked beautiful to Dave and Harlan as she sat in the buggy, very proper, with gloves on her hands and a big floppy hat. "Don't you boys leave here without dropping into Lil's place," she said, looking at Cassidy as she spoke. "That's one place you're always welcome."

She drove away and the outlaws had some comments about the invitation. "She's a humdinger," Kilpatrick said. "Can't go wrong there, fellars. She got some gals up at her place that'll knock your eyes out."

"We done spent most of our money," another observed sadly. "Got to hit the trail and fatten the bank account."

The outlaws were standing now, preparing to leave. Dave asked: "Anybody here know a man name of Lawton Gary?"

All of them suspended all movement, staring silently at Dave, owl-eyed, waiting.

Finally, Cassidy nodded. "Served time with him at Rawlins," he said. "Kind of a blowhard. Bragged he was in jail for robbing a bank. Turned out he was in the hoosegow for killing sheep."

A rumble of laughter went through the crowd.

"Why do you ask?"

"Just wondered if anyone here had rode with him," Dave said quietly.

Cassidy shook his head. "Gary wasn't one to attract too many friends," he said. He took off his new hat and punched out the crown and creased it again. He looked at Longabaugh and Lay and said, "Maybe we better be moving, boys. We got business elsewhere."

"Need any he'p?" Harvey Logan asked quickly.

"This is a three-man operation, Harve. Sorry."

Kilpatrick gazed after Cassidy and his two buddies as they rode away. "He don't want no trigger-happy guns like you an' me with him, Harve."

Dave and Harlan rode out, after Cassidy and his two buddies were out of sight. They made their way to Denver where they sold their horses and enlisted in the Army. Less than twenty-four hours later they were on a train, en route to Tampa, Florida, and the war with Spain.

Day was breaking over the plains below the foothills when Coppers sighted the big pine tree where a faint dirt road took off from the main road. The tree, with all limbs growing on the south side of the trunk, did resemble, from a distance, an Indian war bonnet. He stopped the buckskin and considered the terrain, all the old memories crowding back, not in a haunting way, for a certain comfort had settled on him. He was on home ground. He and Harlan had ridden this way time and again, and while there were some surprises, he was familiar with the lay of the land.

The road, more like a trail, curved westward over grassy hills with the dark hulk of the mountains beyond etched against a deep blue sky. He sent the horse along the trail, noting that nothing had been over the twin traces since the last sprinkle of rain left minuscule craters in the loose dirt. He went past the hills where gold seekers had dug prospect holes sometime in the past, climbed a steepening incline, and dipped down into the valley where Max Callum, the retired railroad detective, had homesteaded a hundred and sixty acres and tried raising horses.

Some time later he surveyed the blackened area where Callum's cabin had stood. Only the stone chimney remained, along with an iron bedstead and cookstove and a few things of melted metal. The barn, which had been a small one, now was a rectangle of ashes. He rode closer, glad that no animals had been in the barn that he could tell. A few scrawny chickens scratched in the dirt around where the cabin had stood, ignoring him as he sat his horse, wondering if what had happened here had anything to do with Harlan Gage's murder back in Cheyenne.

His saddle creaked as he went to the ground, dropping the reins and walking to where the cabin wall had been, squatting to finger the cold ashes. No way of telling how long ago this had happened, no more than why it happened. He scuffed through the black ashes to the bedstead. Once a man had slept here. His bones had been almost entirely consumed by the fire. A charred skull stared blankly from a piece of buffalo robe that had resisted the flames. Dave leaned down to look closely, not touching it, but seeing the small round hole just above the right eye socket. Max Callum had been shot before fire razed his home.

Abruptly, Coppers stood erect. He went back to the buckskin. "Looks like we're stuck with each other, Bucky," he said. "Especially since your replacement has been driven away with all of Callum's other horses." Mounting, Coppers struck out across country, knowing just about where he'd hit the Rafter G ranch road, though now it would be the Slash B.

Long after nightfall, Coppers camped in a swale, where he found grass and creek water. He put the buckskin on a picket line, noting that Gage had provided him with a well-worn lariat. Everything in character, he thought, dumping the saddle on the ground; the leather was cracking and curling, held together with remnants of a piggin string and rawhide.

Making a small fire, he brought water from the creek and put the pot on to boil for coffee. He was examining his saddlebags to find out what Gage had provided in the way of food, when he heard the sound of an approaching horse. He got to his feet and stood outside the circle of light, looking in the direction of the hoofbeats.

The tall shape of a rider on a showy white horse loomed out of the darkness. The rider stopped his horse, shoved his hat on the back of his head, and held up his hand.

"Howdy, neighbor," he said genially. "Had enough ridin' for one day? Well, I sure have." He sat his saddle easily and, in the light of the campfire, Coppers could see a young man, wearing showy clothing to match the trappings of his horse.

"I'm Gil Tatum," he announced. "Mind if I light here and warm a little fodder?"

"It's a free country," Coppers said, stepping back into the firelight.

Gil Tatum laughed. "That it is and for that I give thanks every day o' my life. You headin' for Yellowstone, too?"

"No."

Tatum dismounted and unloosed his cinch and removed the heavy silver-mounted saddle. The buckskin stopped grazing to examine the white horse as Coppers made a quick appraisal of its rider: hat, too large, Coppers thought, spurs too long, too much silver on his batwing chaps and leather vest. This young man was a dude cowboy, but he rode well and seemed at ease. His smile, open and friendly, reminded Coppers of a tail-wagging puppy.

"Got only one cup," Coppers said.

"Thass all right. I got my own gear." Tatum carried his heavy saddle a safe distance from the fire and carefully placed it on the ground. He hobbled the white with practiced ease and, stripping the bridle from the horse, shooed it away.

"Nice-lookin' horse," Gil Tatum said, inviting a comment on his showy horse.

Coppers obliged. "You got the best of it there."

Tatum broke out a tin cup. "Coffee smells like it's done," he said with satisfaction.

Coppers filled their cups and they squatted before the fire, facing one another across the flames, each weighing the other in the manner of strangers on the trail. Tatum liked what he saw.

"I'm headin' up Yellowstone way," Tatum said, blowing on the coffee and taking quick little sips between words. "Gonna get a job with a packhorse outfit, riding dudes around an' showin' them the country."

Coppers nodded.

"Could a went to work for Scott Tyrell—or Will Talbot, for that matter—but I'm not hirin' out as no gunslinger. There's bad blood 'tween them two. Tyrell's the cattleman and ol' Will Talbot runs sheep. You hear 'bout them?"

Coppers shook his head.

"Talbot's meanest ol' sumbitch in the country. I got nothin' against sheep, unnerstan'? I jus' wouldn't work for Will Talbot 'less I was starvin' an' maybe not then. Scott Tyrell ain't much better.

"Seems as how they need dude wranglers up around Yellowstone. Lots o' dudes takin' vacations an' gotta be watched like lil newborn calves.

"Look, I might even go on down to California after I get through at Yellowstone. I hear a feller can make as much as five dollars a day jus' for ridin' an' fallin' off a horse now and then in motion pictures. You believe that?"

"Times they are a-changing," Coppers said.

"You look like you'd make a good wrangler. Why don't you ride with me to Yellowstone? I don't much like travelin' alone."

"I got business the other way," Coppers said.

"Yeah, well, that's how it goes." He sighed and placed his cup on the ground. "I'm gonna rustle up some grub. How d' you like your steak?"

Coppers looked startled and stared at Tatum. The young man grinned widely. "What it rilly is, is beans and bacon," he said. "I got enough for both o' us."

Coppers sat back on the ground, folded his arms around his knees and sipped his coffee. Tatum was a likable young man and reminded him of Harlan Gage, when Harlan was that age. Coppers sensed the rise of feeling, an indescribable loss, thinking about Harlan.

Tatum got supplies from his saddlebags. He sliced potatoes

into the frying pan and added bacon chunks. While this was cooking and sending odors into the surrounding night, he occasionally stirred the pan with his sheath knife, humming a range ditty. He broke out a tin pan and evenly divided the food in the pan and passed it to Dave. "I'll eat outta the fry pan," he said.

They ate in silence. Afterward, Coppers took the utensils down to the creek and scrubbed them out with sand. He returned to the fire to find that Tatum had spread his blanket roll and was lying on it, on his side, his feet to the fire, smoking a cigarette.

Coppers brought his own war bag to the fire and dropped it and scouted the ground, where he intended to spread his blanket, to remove rocks and sticks that might interfere with his sleep. He heard the sodden thunk that brought a flash of the long-forgotten memory of San Juan Hill, and the sound was drowned in the spiteful crack of a rifle. Tatum's body moved convulsively and settled back to the ground as Coppers scrambled away from the fire. Squatting there in the darkness, he searched the area from which the shot had come. All was darkness and the only sound, the whisper of the wind in the brush and the almost inaudible murmur of the creek.

Moving slowly, Coppers headed in the general direction from which the shot had been fired, his pistol ready. He blundered into a mass of thorny vines and backed away.

Hearing the pound of a running horse, he stopped in midstride, turning toward the sound of a horse going from a standstill to a full gallop. In the few moments it took to free himself from the brambles, the sounds of the hard-running horse died away. The red eye of the campfire seemed to beckon and he returned, telling himself he'd not be diverted by anything from the job that lay ahead of him.

Kneeling beside Tatum and hopelessly feeling for a pulse, he, like many another man who'd gone to war, had had his fill of violent death. Tatum had been shot through the head, the large-caliber (Coppers judged it to be a .44-.40 bullet entering an inch below Tatum's right eye and emerging from the back of his head. He'd died instantly.

Coppers stared down at Tatum, wondering why Tatum was

killed and he was spared. A single shot, out of the dark; the killer could have as easily picked off both men.

Considering what little he knew of Tatum, he decided almost at once that Gil Tatum was not an outlaw. He was, Coppers believed, exactly as he presented himself: ambitious, adventurous, devil-may-care, a youth who inspired immediate trust and liking. A brush-jumper, a man on the run, was a conservative man in dress, Coppers had found. An outlaw didn't attract attention to himself with garish clothing. Most of them rode bays and blacks, a coloration that blended with the environment, merging with the terrain when viewed in the distance.

No, Tatum was not an outlaw.

With a heavy heart, Coppers saddled the flashy white horse, lifted Tatum across the rig, and secured his body to the saddle. He saddled Bucky and took one last look around the camp before kicking dirt on the dying fire. He mounted Bucky, gathered the lead lines of the white horse, and headed for Arapaho, the nearest town in his line of travel.

CHAPTER SIX

Coppers reached Arapaho just before midnight, reined his horse in at the dark building with a sign that read: TOWN MARSHAL. He could see lights in only two other buildings in town, both saloons. The white horse whinnied and Bucky answered.

Dismounting, he tied both animals to the hitch rail. There seemed to be a note nailed to the door. He crossed the short porch and struck a match, leaning close but unable to read the illegible scrawl which appeared to have been there since the building was constructed.

About to turn away, he heard a snort and a blubbering snore beyond the walls. He tried the door and found it to be unlocked. Leaning inside the dark room, which smelled of sweat and gun oil, he tried to pierce the gloom, calling, "Anybody here?"

Coppers was answered by another snort and the creaking of a bed. "Yeah, jussa minute." A match flared and Coppers saw an old man with short white whiskers sitting on the edge of a cot of Army issue. He was dressed in red flannel underwear and squinted from the light of the dying match. Some faint remembrance of this man stirred in Coppers' brain.

"I'll light the lamp," Coppers said, striking a match on his thumbnail and walking to a rolltop desk in one corner of the small office. Lifting the glass chimney, he put the match to the wick, adjusted the flame, and replaced the globe. He turned around and it came to him at once that this man was Al Hunter, the one-time door shaker in Laramie, when Coppers was a kid. The last time Coppers had seen Al Hunter was on the day his parents had been brutally murdered. It was plain to Coppers that Al Hunter didn't remember him; after all, Coppers thought, I was only about ten or eleven years old.

The old man's head came up. He had a gleam in his eyes of annoyance or expectation. "What's wrong now, mister?"

"You're the town marshal?"

Hunter shook his head in denial. "Town ain't had no marshal, not since the last one tried to stop a ruckus. I'm detailed from the county seat, deputy sheriff I am, and responsible for law an' order hereabouts. What's it you want?"

"Fellow named Gil Tatum outside there, dead. He was shot from ambush over on the Little Medicine Creek."

"When did this happen?"

"Just after dark last night."

"And you brung the body here?" The old man had a hint of a whine in his voice. "Couldn't you a took him some other place?"

"Arapaho was nearest to where it happened."

"Got any idea who blowed away your friend?"

"He's not my friend," Coppers said irritably. "I was making camp for the night when he rode in and asked if he could share my fire. I never saw him before last night."

Hunter heaved himself to his feet and took one step and backed up and sat down again. He reached under the cot and brought out his boots and laboriously pulled them on while Coppers waited, his impatience mounting.

Finally, the old man stood up again, still in his long johns with a baggy seat, stamping his feet. He walked unsteadily to the desk, lifted the lamp, and held it waveringly. He thrust the lamp out to Coppers. "Here, you hold this dang thing. I'm a mite shaky."

Coppers took the lamp and led the way outside. He went close to the white horse, holding the lamp aloft.

Hunter wheezed up behind him. "Sure got a purty hoss," he said. He leaned down to look into Gil Tatum's face. "Ah, God, that bullet jes' about took his head off! Whoinell would kill a nice-lookin' young feller like that?" He glanced up at Coppers. "Where'd you say he's from?"

"I didn't say because I don't know," Coppers said. "He told me he was going to Yellowstone to work for a trail-riding outfit, taking care of dudes on vacation. After that, he said something about going to California to work in motion pictures, whatever that is."

"He could a been in a Wild West show," Hunter observed. "All them fancy duds. You get a look at the killer?"

"No. I heard him ride away after he fired that one shot. Too dark to do any tracking."

Hunter shook his head, straightened, groaning and putting his two hands on his back. "You're new here. Workin' for Tyrell or Talbot?"

"Neither," Coppers said. "Passing through."

Hunter squinted at him, looking at him steadily. "I can smell law a mile away. You a lawman? You ever been a lawman?"

Coppers shook his head. "Just a saddle tramp."

"Humph! Well—you better stick around till I get a chance to ride out and look over the ground where Tatum was shot."

"I can't do that," Coppers said. "I've got to be on my way."

"In a hurry, air ye? Well, I guess if worse comes to worse I could lock you up as a material witness. Trouble is, I got two sheepherders in jail now on a murder charge and the damn jail is plumb full."

"I'd planned to stop off at the Slash B," Coppers said reluctantly. "If need be, you can reach me there."

"Boynton's place, huh? Gonna go to work there?"

"I may. I don't know yet."

"Well, they're a mighty quar bunch out there. Kinda whacko, the whole lot, even the hired help."

Coppers hesitated. "You mentioned holding a couple of sheepherders. Is there a cattle-sheep war going on?"

"You betcha boots, two o' the biggest wheels goin' at it hammer and tongs."

"Who's winning?"

Hunter snorted. "Nobody wins them kind, no sir!"

Coppers placed the wind-flickered lamp in Hunter's shaky hands. "That's the reason you're outstationed here?"

"Yep, that's it. Keeps me doggone busy, I mean. I thought you mighta been bringin' me bad tidin's about Tyrell and Talbot, the two who's raisin' hell."

Coppers untied his horse and mounted. "See you, Deputy," he said, and reined Bucky away.

"Hey, wait a minute, what's your name?" Hunter called.

Coppers didn't respond but kept riding out the way he'd entered town. He glanced back once to see Deputy Al Hunter holding the lamp and staring after him.

Not a hell of a good beginning, he thought glumly and not for the first time.

CHAPTER SEVEN

You are losing them all, Dave Coppers told himself along about nooning. He'd been close to three murders—Gage, Max Callum, and now the painfully young Gil Tatum. Was there a connection between the three? he asked himself.

He had an instinctive feeling that there was something very important that he should know. And didn't know, couldn't even guess. He found the thought aggravating, refusing to be put aside, out of mind, as he could usually do.

He had taught himself to take things as they came, doing the most important task first and being able to sort out what actually was most important and what was inconsequential. From the start this operation had given him a convincing feeling that something had been left out.

His job was to find out who was bringing genuine currency (but with a forged official signature) into the market place. That was the main objective to be sure. But that elusive, tantalizing, and frustrating indefinable something nagged at him despite his effort to put the whole mess out of his mind.

His shadow was black on the ground directly under him when he stopped by a creek to let Bucky drink. He lay flat on his belly upstream from the horse and sucked in the sweet, cold water. He saw a pad then, imprinted in the sand and gravel, of a big cat, as big a track as he'd ever looked at. He whistled softly as he studied the track and the ones leading away from it. The cougar had been crippled, for the left hind pad barely indented the soft sand of the creek, while the other three went deep, indicating a heavy animal.

He went to the saddle and put the buckskin across the creek, keeping a wary eye on his surrounds as well as tracking the big cat. He got a glimpse of the tawny shape going through mountain mahogany on the slope above him, and perhaps an hour's ride from ranch headquarters as he remembered them.

A movement caught his eye. A horseman, just below the stalking cat, seemed unaware of his danger. The strange stance of the rider puzzled him at first and then with a soft oath he realized it was a woman—even though she rode astride. He reached for the Winchester saddle gun and at the same time shouted a warning as the big cat began his bounding charge. The woman's horse sensed danger and spun about in a sudden motion that almost unseated the rider.

The cat came on, tail switching, gaining speed despite the crippled leg. Probably an old mama, he thought, raising the rifle. The woman's horse pitched and bucked into the rifle sight and Coppers muttered a curse. Jamming the rifle back into the boot, he put spurs to the startled buckskin and shook out a big loop in the lariat as he went ahead. The buckskin accepted the whirling loop and Coppers had a moment to thank Gage for picking a roping-wise horse.

The cat leaped, its claws digging in the rump of the woman's horse. The horse squealed in terror and kicked high but failed to dislodge the cat. Coppers made his cast as the cat, clawing savagely to maintain its hold, slipped farther back. The loop went high and beyond, but the horse bucked into a gnarled cedar, knocking the rider off. The movement of the horse brought the cat under the loop which settled on a forepaw. The buckskin felt the rope tighten and slid to a halt, jerking the cat to the ground. Bucky backed, keeping tension on the rope. The big cat came directly at Coppers, mouth wide, teeth exposed, snarling. Coppers had no time to lever the rifle. He jerked out his pistol and fired, hitting the cougar in the right shoulder, causing the tawny beast to slide sideways, offering a better target. Coppers shot again, hitting the cougar inches behind the right shoulder, dropping it to the ground.

Coppers dismounted and quieted the trembling buckskin. The woman's horse had disappeared over a low ridge, galloping wildly, stirrups flapping.

He tied Bucky to a low bush and strode to the woman, who lay face down beside the trail, under the split cedar. She wore a pair of tight-fitting Levis and a shirtwaist of some filmy material

that Coppers found most attractive. Her broad-brimmed black
hat lay near her outstretched hand. Coppers didn't know too
much about women, but he classed this one instinctively as thor-
oughbred, with her finely honed features, her dark eyelashes
lying against her healthily tanned cheek.

He scrubbed the wiry black stubble on his scarred face and
leaned forward, turning her gently, shoving his hand under her
head. Her eyes remained closed but she breathed softly. A thin
trickle of blood had traced a mark down one smooth brown
cheek. He ruffled her hair, seeing where the cedar limb had
struck her just above her ear. He carefully lifted her in his arms,
astonished at how light she was, and carried her to a grassy knoll
beside the trail.

He went to his horse and lifted his canteen from the saddle.
He came back to the woman; the buckskin settled down and
began grazing.

Young—young, and pretty, Coppers thought, as he let water
trickle into her mouth. He sprinkled a few drops on her face and
sponged them off with his neckerchief.

Her dark wavy hair fell to her shoulders, her eyebrows an inky
arch, her features beautifully chiseled. He wondered at the color
her eyes might be. He wondered, too, what she'd think when she
saw him for the first time. Shrink back, maybe. Some women did
and some men, too, even when he didn't have a few days of
black stubble on his face.

The girl stirred and slowly opened her eyes. They were a
shade of cool gray, shadowed by the dusky long lashes. When
she tried to raise herself, Coppers said, "Take it easy, you'll be
all right." He encircled her shoulders to steady her. She didn't
pull away or shrink from him. She put out her hand and touched
his face briefly, and Coppers felt a funny, strange feeling go all
through his body.

She murmured, "You're a stranger," smiled, and tried to get
up. Coppers offered his hand but had to take her arm to help her
to her feet.

"I'll help you," he said.

Still smiling at him, her teeth very white against the smooth
brown of her face, she looked at him and yet looked beyond, un-
seeing.

She said, "If you'll catch up my horse, please. . . ."

Coppers gazed at her and a great flood of pity welled up in him. "I'm sorry, ma'am," he said. "I didn't know—" he hesitated, not wanting to say the word.

She wavered and steadied herself on his arm. "You didn't know I'm blind?" she asked lightly. "Well, how could you?"

Coppers felt almost glad for a moment that she couldn't see him as he looked and then was enveloped with a sense of shame for the thought.

"If you'll bring up my horse, please," she repeated.

"Sorry. He spooked after that cat clawed him."

She shivered. "She's a mare, not a he. . . . Was that what attacked me? I could hear it growling and I was terrified, even more than Farah, my mare." She moved closer to him. "What happened to the—cat?"

"Dead," Coppers said briefly. "She was desperate for food or else she'd never have went for you."

"She? A mother cat?"

"A dry one," Coppers said.

"Dry? What does that mean?"

"No cubs. She was an old one, ma'am, with one good tooth and crippled in one leg."

"I'm glad there aren't babies to starve to death. How'll I get home?" She laughed and said, "Excuse me, my name is Aletha Boynton."

"I'm Dave," he said. "You—my horse will take you there."

"Will your horse ride double?"

"I wouldn't want to try him out right now," Coppers said. "Anyway, he's come a long way on grass. I'll walk." Her concern for the horse touched him. "I'll be with you soon's I get my rope off the cat."

He walked to the cat, unloosed the lariat and coiled it up; he returned to the buckskin and hung the rope on his saddle, feeling a twinge of uncertainty. He'd never been a devious man, and deceit, however trivial, troubled him.

He said, "All right," and lifted her to the saddle and asked her if she felt all right.

She nodded, smiling, and said, "You're kind; thank you."

He nodded and then said, "You're welcome." He held the

reins and walked beside the buckskin; the woman's small booted foot brushed his arm now and then as her body moved to the motion of the horse. He looked up into her face and saw that she still smiled. She's a happy person, he thought, wondering why, unable to see the sunrise and sunset, the mountains, the trees, she seemed sufficient, giving off an aura of happiness and contentment. He refused to think of what her role in the counterfeiting might be.

"We live on the old Rafter G," she said. "My grandfather and I. It's the Slash B now." Her voice had a throaty, almost breathless quality that spoke of enthusiasm for living. "You may stay at the ranch and rest up. Or you could work there if you wanted to." Her hand rested for a moment on Coppers' shoulder and he felt the same strange feeling he'd experienced when she touched his face. Or maybe it was because he'd fallen into a lucky spot for his impending search. If the Slash B *was* headquarters for the gang.

"I do want to show I'm grateful to you."

"It's my pleasure," Coppers said.

"If you'd consider it," she said, "I'm sure that Lute—he's our foreman—could use you. He's always complaining about not enough help."

Coppers was silent, thinking of the few, very few, cattle he'd seen thus far—scrawny, ladder-ribbed, most of them without calves. The drift fence, too, he remembered, was down in several places, the posts rotting, wire sagging. The irrigation ditches, overgrown with weeds and brush, seemed a forlorn testimonial to neglect and decay.

Coppers stopped the buckskin. Ahead of them, three horsemen broke over the swell of earth, leading the mare which apparently had headed for the ranch after being clawed and bitten. Not slackening their pace, the riders ran their horses hard right at them.

"That's the crew," Aletha said.

The hoofbeats built up, and the three men, when a dozen feet away, stopped as though on command, horses' hooves stamping, bridle chains jingling.

A big man on a gray edged his horse closer, his dark brown

face impassive, his icy-blue eyes on Coppers only, probing suspiciously. He had his look and turned his eyes on Aletha.

"We worried, Miss Boynton," he said, and his eyes now curious and challenging went back to Coppers. He swept his hat from his head and swabbed his face with his neckerchief, his blond curls glistening in the sun. "Your horse come in with blood on her rump." He replaced his hat and continued, "You shouldn't be out riding alone, Miss Aletha, like I told you before." As he spoke his eyes remained on Coppers.

"Ah, Lute," she said, "I'd die if I stayed at the ranch all the time."

"Sure, sure," Lute interrupted. "Any one of us would be glad to ride with you. Whenever you want."

There was a stubborn tilt to her chin as she said, "Lute, this is Dave. He rescued me from a poor, starving old cougar. Dave, Lute. He's the Slash B foreman and he thinks I should stay home all the time."

"That'd be hard to do," Coppers said.

Lute Farnell scowled, staring at Coppers. The two men locked gazes without friendliness, each measuring the other. Coppers didn't like what he looked at and didn't bother to conceal it. Too damn good-looking, Coppers thought sourly, and arrogant as a prize bull.

The two men who rode with Farnell stirred. One of them spoke: "If'n it's all right with you, boss, we'll go on back." He was whiskery gray, snaggletoothed, and tobacco juice stained his chin.

Some faint memory stirred in Coppers' brain as he covertly looked at the man, trying to remember where he'd seen him.

Farnell nodded. "Go on, Dakota. You and Slim can find something to do 'round the home place for the rest of the day." He dismissed them with a wave of his hand as he swung down and put his hands on Aletha's slim waist. "I brought your horse."

"That horse has been hurt," Coppers said. "Shouldn't be rode till she's been looked at." He glanced at the two cowhands riding away at a lope, ordinary-appearing men who wouldn't have been out of place on any working ranch.

Aletha firmly removed Lute's hands from her waist. "He's right, Lute. I'll ride here and I'll be all right." She turned her head toward Coppers. "Dave'll be with us for a while. He'll decide later on if he'll work for us."

Lute Farnell's face darkened with fury. But when he spoke his voice was smooth and unruffled. "As you wish," he said. "I'll ride on, Aletha, because with that fella walking you'll be quite a spell." He mounted his horse, dug in his spurs, and ran his mount hard away from them.

It was then that Coppers remembered. Dakota was one of those outlaws at Steamboat Springs. He'd brought Butch Cassidy a hat from the general store to replace the derby Butch was wearing the first time Coppers laid eyes on him.

Coppers and Gage had had only a fleeting contact with Dakota, but Dave was troubled. Had Dakota recognized him?

CHAPTER EIGHT

Striding along beside the buckskin, Coppers thought about Farnell. The man was antagonistic at once, no doubt about that, though he'd successfully concealed it from Aletha. Coppers considered whether Farnell would have the brains and know-how to run an operation such as that necessary to forge signatures and distribute bank notes. How, he wondered, could one measure another's intelligence, cunning, or whatever? He glanced up at the lovely woman riding his horse. She trusted Farnell, obviously. That must count for something.

"Have you always been—were you—?" He stopped, feeling that he was asking for information he should not have.

"Oh, no, you don't have to be so sensitive, Dave. My blindness was caused by an accident."

"You don't have to tell me."

"I know. Everyone seems so sympathetic when they learn. I've managed to get along very well. I do most things that sighted people do."

"I'm sure you do."

"But you don't believe me! Well, that accident should not have happened. Farah, my mare has been trained to follow that circuit which gives me an hour's ride. It was the cat and probably an unusual incident."

"I've never heard of a cougar attacking a human before," Coppers acknowledged. "But this one was old and very hungry."

"At any other time Farah could have outrun the cat."

Coppers didn't tell her how the cat had stalked and attacked the horse. "She appears to be fast," Coppers said mildly.

Aletha laughed again and touched his shoulder with her hand. "When I was thirteen my parents and I were visiting Grandfather. He had a cabin down at Piney Point, on the Chesapeake

Bay. We went sailing, my mother and father and I. A storm came up, a terrible storm, like a tornado, and blew the mast right off. The mast fell and hit me. I lost consciousness and when I came to, the boat was gone. So were my parents. I lost my eyesight shortly thereafter."

"Good Lord," Coppers muttered. He raised his voice, "I'm sorry, very sorry." He was silent for a moment, thinking of what she'd told him. "How did you get ashore?"

"I had a life jacket. My mother and father didn't."

The road Coppers remembered so well cut across a low ridge above the ranch. They crested the swell and Coppers stopped and the buckskin stopped. Coppers stared. The old ranch house was gone and in its place stood a handsome two-story stone building. The barn and outbuildings were the same but the main house stood out like a castle.

"What's the matter?" Aletha asked.

"We're on the ridge just above the ranch," Coppers said. "Sure a beautiful place."

She smiled, pleased. "Grandfather knew just what he wanted. I'm glad you like it."

They went on then, past the corrals, the barn and outbuildings. Coppers stopped the horse in front of the house and helped Aletha down. An ancient black man came from the house and took charge of Aletha.

Coppers watched them inside and then went to the bunkhouse, leading the buckskin. He got his pack from behind the cantle and dropped the sack beside the bunkhouse steps. He led the buckskin to the barn, where he gave the animal a thorough rubdown before turning it into a box stall with a generous helping of grain. After filling the manger with hay he went back to where he'd dropped his war sack. He was stooping to pick it up when Farnell spoke from behind him.

"Just leave it there, cowboy," Farnell said, his voice even and cold.

Coppers straightened with the bedroll in his left hand, turning slowly. He looked into Farnell's cold blue eyes for a moment, then shrugged, letting the war sack slip from his fingers.

Farnell smiled thinly and there was a contemptuous lift of his lips. "Course we'll expect you to eat before you move on," he said mockingly. He put his horse toward the barn. Coppers watched him as he rode his horse into the barn, then he turned into the bunkhouse.

The small, thin man Farnell had called Dakota sat cross-legged on his bunk. He uncurled his feet and stood up. "Howdy," he said with a friendly snaggletooth grin. "Don't pay too much 'tention to Lute. He's all keyed up 'bout Miz Boynton."

The other man, a slender, stoop-shouldered cowboy with a deep scar on his jaw said, "Shet up, Dakota. You're alluz shootin' off your big yap when you oughta keep quiet."

Dakota winked at Coppers slyly. "Ain't no law ag'n talkin', is there, Slim?"

"If there was, you'd be doin' time," Slim growled and stalked outside.

"Sure a sociable place," Coppers said. He stroked the dark stubble on his face. "Got a razor, Dakota? Lost mine somewhere along the trail." He'd thought he'd let his beard grow, but after meeting Aletha he changed his mind, telling himself, how will she know if you shave or not? No matter. It'd make him feel better.

Dakota waved his hand. "Ain't got one o' my own," he said. "Lute's got one an' I'll get it for you."

"Better not," Coppers advised. "Lute won't like it."

Dakota was rummaging around on a shelf and before Coppers could protest further the old man put a razor in his hand.

"Hop to it," he chuckled. "Lute won't mind a-tall."

Coppers shrugged and peeled off to his waist. He went to the back porch, shaving by a small, cloudy mirror tacked to the wall. He washed his face and dried himself. He stood on the porch a moment, watching the sun dip toward the familiar rugged mountains and for a moment a good feeling came over him with a note of promise. He went back in the bunkhouse and gave the razor to Dakota. Farnell entered, followed by Slim. Farnell stopped, swung around, his eyes narrowed. "Damn it, that's my razor," he said.

"Don't get your dobber up, Lute," Dakota drawled. "I lent it to him."

"You got a hell of a nerve, lending something doesn't belong to you."

"Now, now, Lute," Dakota said placatingly, yet his voice was tinged with irony.

Coppers could feel the violence in the air. His pistol belt hung on a bunk post ten feet away, and that was as distant as the mountains.

Farnell relaxed suddenly, a smile appearing on his face, however forced. "All right," he said. "Guess a man has to shave once in a while." He went to his bunk and sat on it. Slim silently seated himself on an adjoining bunk. Both men quietly watched Coppers as he slipped into a clean shirt.

"What sheriff you dodging?" Farnell said.

"Probably the same one you are," Coppers answered.

Dakota laughed silently and Farnell laid angry eyes on him but that didn't stop the old man.

There was an uncertain, timid knock on the door and it opened slowly. The old Negro whom Coppers had seen earlier stepped hesitantly into the room.

"What the hell you want here, Wash?" Farnell demanded to know. "You know I don't like you comin' here."

Wash looked around without speaking until his eyes rested on Coppers. "Miz Boynton say you come to supper," he said. "We ready eat in ten minutes." He bent stiffly and backed to the door, his eyes rolling fearfully in Farnell's direction.

Dakota tittered. "Hee, hee, guess ol' Lute's gonna get some competish, hee, hee, hee."

"Shut up, you damned old fool," Farnell said. "You know I don't allow blacks in my bunkhouse." He came off his bunk and strode to confront Coppers, his face hardening.

"I want no trouble, Farnell," Coppers said. "What I do want and need is real food I guess that old fellow can cook up. I've lived on jackrabbits too long."

"You look it," said Farnell, "all but that fancy hat. Where'd you get it?"

"What's wrong with my hat?"

"Don't match the rest o' your outfit," Farnell declared.

"I picked it up by mistake," Coppers said cautiously. He steeled himself to take Farnell's insults because if he called the man all bets would be off.

"Yeah, yeah," Farnell said disbelievingly. "The previous owner's probably lyin' somewhere with a bullet in him."

"You hadn't orter say things like that, Lute," Dakota said.

"Your strings gonna run out one of these days, old man," Farnell said. But he walked back to his bunk and seated himself.

"It's gonna run out fer all o' us," Dakota said.

Coppers got his gunbelt from the bunk post and strapped it on, feeling better almost at once. Farnell was upset by Coppers' appearance on the ranch, that was plain to see. The foreman represented the type of man Coppers held little regard for, and he was galled to be forced to accept the man's obvious attempt to force a fight. Under different circumstances he'd be glad to oblige.

He nodded at them all and walked out of the bunkhouse, glad to be out of there and in the fast-chilling night. He breathed deep of the high thin air and his expelling breath sounded with relief. The tension in the bunkhouse was heavy. There was an undercurrent of hate and violence there.

Coppers mounted the steps to the porch that ran full-length, on the two sides of the main house. A porch swing swayed idly in the breeze at one end of the porch. He could smell the tang of the pine and sage and wild country on the wind.

Wash answered his knock, opening the door with a bow. "Sorry, suh," he said, low-voiced, pointing to Coppers' gunbelt. "Miz Boynton, she—well, she jes' can't stan' them things in the house."

Coppers shrugged. "Uh, how'll she know?" he asked.

Wash smiled, showing an expanse of even white teeth. "I don't know how she know, boss, but she sho' do know."

Coppers shook his head. "You got a proddy bunch around here, Wash," he said. "I wouldn't feel safe without my gun."

"Sho', boss, you be all right in heah. Lemme take it in my kitchen. When you leave, I gives it to you."

"Good enough," Coppers said reluctantly as he unbuckled his gunbelt and passed it to the black.

"Right in here, sir," Wash said, and padded through the house. He placed Coppers' gunbelt on a table and opened a door off the hallway. "Raht through heah, suh."

Coppers went into the room, smelling a faint scent of violets.

Aletha, he thought. He viewed the room quickly, taking in the colorful Indian rugs covering the entire floor, and some hanging from the walls. Rough but comfortable hand-hewn furniture gave the room a simple elegance. A small fire blazed in the big stone fireplace at the end of the large room. An elderly man sat in a wheelchair beside the fireplace. His hair and beard, snow white, gleamed in the firelight as he motioned Coppers forward.

"Welcome to the Slash B, stranger," he said in a soft and courteous drawl. "You're the man who assisted Aletha, I take it?"

The old man's grip didn't reveal severe weakness, Coppers thought. He said, "Anyone would be proud to help her, Mr. Boynton."

Boynton peered at him from beneath bushy white brows, his pale blue eyes lively and alert. "Not so sure of that," he said. "Maybe fifteen, twenty years ago . . . We got a new breed coming into this country. Not like in the old days." He raised his head and his voice: "Washington, oh, Washington, come here right now."

"Yes, suh," Washington said, standing attentively before the old man.

Boynton looked at Coppers. "Would you care for a drink before supper is served?"

Coppers nodded. Things didn't fit here. Except for the place the Boyntons lived in, this rundown old ranch with its ramshackle outbuildings and rotting fences and evidence of deterioration, didn't add up. No cattle or hay, to speak of, that Coppers had been able to discover. He wondered where the money came from. He was still cogitating, only half listening to Boynton when Washington brought small glasses of dark wine.

Boynton raised his glass, toasting Coppers' well-being and happiness. Coppers sipped the wine, finding it dry and tingly, soothing to his throat. His belly griped hungrily as the wine warmed his body.

Boynton's head swung around and Coppers turned. Aletha Boynton came down the staircase, her hand on the bannister, head erect and smiling. Coppers wondered if she always smiled and if it was put there to cover up her blindness.

Coppers ached inside at the beauty of Aletha. Dressed in white, a filmy thing that outlined her shapely figure, her firm young breasts, slender waist and full hips, she reminded him of a royal princess. Coppers unconsciously straightened, holding the tiny wine glass in his big fist, and then he caught the old man's piercing look and he glanced away.

Aletha came on down the stairs and walked to stand beside Coppers. "We're happy to have you with us—and I hope Grandfather didn't talk you to sleep."

"I enjoyed listening to him," Coppers said, wondering what it was the old man had talked about. He couldn't remember.

She took his arm, smiling. "Lute can't sit still when Grandfather starts talking about the good old days."

Coppers felt the warmth of her hand on his arm and wanted it to stay there. He also wanted to rush headlong from the room, conscious of his wrinkled shirt, his dirty Levis and scuffed boots. But most of all he was conscious of his battered and scarred face, wondering what Aletha would think if she could see him.

But she talked happily and Coppers felt her happiness, and her feelings were transmitted to him through some mysterious alchemy. "We're lucky you happened along, Dave. Lute and the boys have been working so hard."

"That man Farnell is a crackerjack," said Boynton as Wash announced dinner and came to push the wheelchair into the dining room. After all of them were seated around the table, Boynton resumed: "We didn't have much when we came out from Virginia and bought this ranch. My health—I thought it'd get better. Did at first, in this high, thin air, and then seems I got worse. Lute's made the ranch pay and that helped. Now he needs another hand, I suspect."

"Shouldn't be hard to pick up good men this time of year," Coppers said, puzzled by Boynton's revelation. If Boynton was the man who made the bad money marketable, would not he side with Lute in wanting to get rid of a stranger?

"We're too far off the beaten path," Aletha said. "Hardly anyone comes by here. Our nearest neighbors, Mel Bennion and his family on the Box MB, are twenty miles from here."

"He should be able to pick up another rider easy enough," Coppers said.

Boynton chuckled. "Lute's mighty hard to please. He won't take on just anybody."

Thinking of Slim, who obviously was a gunslinger, and Dakota, whom he knew to be an old outlaw, the words made no sense to Coppers. He felt a growing sense of frustration which was somewhat quelled with Wash's excellent supper. He was enjoying it as he had never enjoyed a meal before. He realized then, with a start, that Ida Mae Courtney, at the Washington, D.C., boarding home, had consistently served him good food. Must be the altitude, he thought. . . .

Boynton's voice broke in on his thoughts. ". . . and if Lute keeps on raising profits the way he has, Aletha will be able to go back East and see that eye specialist."

Aletha groped for her grandfather's hand and placed her own hand over it. "I'm not sure you should even think about that let alone talk of it."

"You mean she would be able—" Coppers stopped.

"Yes, it's possible that with a certain operation now available Aletha could see again. Not me, though; I'm too old. It'd be a waste of money."

This was the first inkling Coppers had that the old man's vision was impaired. But if Boynton couldn't see, how could he manage to doctor paper money? Coppers looked up to find the old man with an expectant look on his face, as he waited for an answer.

"Sorry, I missed your question," Coppers said.

"I asked if you intend to remain with us." He motioned to Wash and the black man wheeled the chair back into the living room, and Coppers and Aletha followed. She went to the organ and seated herself and began to play a soft, haunting song not familiar to Coppers. He stood with his back to the fire and carefully fashioned a cigarette.

Coppers knew he'd stay on at the Slash B if the opportunity allowed it. It seemed that such would happen, considering both Aletha and Boynton's invitation. He had many doubts about this remote ranch being used as headquarters for an unlawful operation, but he assumed not much time would be lost in checking it out. And there was Aletha, who fascinated him.

He stopped in midsentence as a gun was fired in the distance. He looked at Aletha and found her head erect and features alert but not frightened. There was a pause and then three rapid shots boomed, closer yet. Widely spaced shots followed as Coppers ran from the room, looking for Wash, to get his gun.

It sounded as though a pitched battle was going on out there somewhere and not too far away.

He heard Aletha call as Wash came from the kitchen with the gunbelt in his hands. Coppers grabbed the gunbelt and strapped it on as he plunged out the back door into the night. A flash of yellow led him between corrals leading toward the south pasture.

CHAPTER NINE

Gunshots blasted the night, re-echoing among the hills, as Coppers, crouching and moving, circled the barn, keeping away from the sagging building so as to get a wider view of the terrain. A yellow flash blooming in the night led him in that direction, his pistol held loosely in his right hand.

He'd taken no more than a dozen steps when another gunshot sounded in another area, a good hundred yards from the first flash.

Stopping short, he scanned the area, puzzled at the occasional shot in the night. Sometimes he'd see a flash of gunpowder and it appeared to flame upward. Someone was firing into the night sky. But why? He remained still, thinking of the lay of the land, most of it coming back to him. The folds of the foothills to the Rockies made an undulating wave on the land. The more rugged terrain higher up drew him and he moved in that direction, not hurrying, alert, in trigger-taut readiness.

He made it to high ground in the immediate area above the barn and knelt in the shadows of a clump of fragrant pine, watching and listening. A long silence was broken by another round of firing in two different areas. Despite his elevation he could see no fire flashes now. He was unsure if the shooters had moved from their original locations.

He waited in heavy silence, looking at the sky now and then, at the position of the Dog Star. When he estimated that half an hour had passed and not another shot fired, he started to rise, only to sink back when he heard stumbling footsteps approaching. The form of a man appeared below him and when he drew near, Coppers cocked his pistol and said, "Hold it right there."

The man stopped deadstill, his hands half raised. "It's me—Slim," he said.

Coppers rose to his feet and moved forward, his pistol ready. "What's going on?"

"I dunno. Heard shootin' an' all and come to see for myself. Me and Dakota."

"Where's Dakota?"

"Dunno. He took one side o' the arroyo and I took the other. Never did find out who's doin' all the shootin'. Maybe rustlers."

Not likely, Coppers thought. There's no cattle to steal; but he did not say that, remaining silent.

At last Coppers spoke: "Get on back to the bunkhouse."

"Don't be tellin' me what to do," Slim grumbled, but he moved away.

Coppers waited until the sound of Slim's passing died away. Here in this exposed place the night was still, the stars bright and seemingly near enough to touch. The slightest sound would carry. He felt a cool wind coming down from higher places as he made his way toward the castle, slowly, and with great care.

Coppers had no thought of listening to a conversation not meant for him. The moment he began this mission he was a changed man in that he made himself consciously more aware of what went on around him. Thus it was that he noiselessly approached the castle and stopped just before rounding the front corner of the house which stood dark and silent, except for the soft rumble of voices and the creaking of the porch swing.

Silent, he moved even closer and heard Lute's voice, plain now: "We're lucky we didn't lose the prize herd in the south pasture, Aletha." His voice sounded sincere, tinged with the right amount of indignation.

"We're the lucky ones," Aletha said in a soft, soft voice, "to have you here, Lute."

Farnell grunted. "Might not be so lucky next time. I tell you, honey, I believe that new fella is working with the rustlers. That's how they do it, send a saddle bum in to size things up—"

"I don't believe that, Lute," Aletha interrupted in a firm voice.

"I know you're beholden to him," Lute said stubbornly. "But I'm not sure it wasn't all planned, every bit of it. Dakota's a good tracker and he saw the cat's tracks and he saw the hoof prints of the stranger's horse. That fella might just have herded that cat right into you—"

"Lute, that's ridiculous!" Aletha exclaimed. "You're so terribly biased about Dave. He's a good man. I can sense it, and I won't stand for you talking like that."

Coppers felt a glow of pleasure at Aletha's defense of him. His feelings about her disturbed him in a manner new to him. Now, his joy died quickly when he thought of Farnell's statement about a prize herd in the south pasture. What kind of game was Farnell playing here? he wondered. And then gave up on conjecture as Farnell argued again.

"You can't be too careful," Farnell said heatedly. "He ain't what he appears to be; I know that for dang sure. Did he tell you anything about himself?"

"Only that he grew up around here."

"I think I ought to encourage him to move on."

"I forbid it," Aletha said briskly. "Both Grandfather and I have asked him to stay—if he so desires. Now, it's up to you, Lute, to make it easy. You can offer him a job—"

"That I won't do," Farnell said angrily. "It wouldn't be in your best interest, Miss Aletha."

"Now it's Miss Aletha," she said quietly. "You're angry, Lute, and I respect your feelings, but I simply must ask you to respect mine, too."

"It's not just me," Farnell said, his voice edged with desperation. "I wasn't goin' to tell you this but I feel I've got to, to make you see it my way. Dakota told me he's sure he's seen this fella somewhere before. You know Dakota used to be a lawman in his younger days. He thinks he might 'a run into this fella in a lawbreaking showdown."

"But he's not sure," Aletha said.

"Well, it was a long time ago. Dakota mentioned he'd seen him someplace but couldn't remember where—"

"That's not enough, Lute. I want you to give Dave the benefit of the doubt." The swing creaked decisively. "It's getting chilly. I'm going inside." Her footsteps sounded on the wood flooring of the porch, slowed and stopped. "Promise me you'll do as I ask, Lute."

He was silent.

"Promise?"

"Ah, well I hope it don't turn out bad," Farnell said with resignation.

"Thank you, Lute," Aletha said.

"Wait a minute, ma'am," Lute said. "Where was this fella when all the shootin' was goin' on?"

She was silent for a long running moment. Then she said, "I don't know, Lute. He ran out the back door after he got his gun from Wash."

"See there!" Lute said heatedly. "I guess maybe—"

"Lute, we'll not discuss it any further," she said and her inflection left no room for argument.

Coppers heard the door open and close. He stood there in silence, listening to Farnell cursing in a low, strangled, rage-filled voice. Then Farnell's boots sounded on the porch, a further clatter as he descended the steps and retreated into the night, toward the bunkhouse.

Long after Aletha entered the castle and long after Farnell's departure, Coppers stood waiting in the darkness. The only visible light was the splash of dim yellow on the ground outside the bunkhouse. The castle itself was dark.

Coppers turned slowly toward the bunkhouse only to come to a sudden halt as a light went on in the castle. He stood there, looking in wonder at the figure of Boynton standing beside the lamp he'd just lighted. The wheelchair was not in sight.

As Dave watched, Boynton lifted the lamp and walked with a firm and steady tread across the room. The light flickered with the movement of Boynton's body and then suddenly the light went out. Trying to remember the layout of the house, Coppers could only surmise that Boynton had descended to a basement, if there was a basement; or that he had entered a ground-floor room which had no windows.

He waited a while longer and then strolled thoughtfully toward the bunkhouse. His war bag still rested on the ground beside the steps. He picked it up, slung it over his shoulder, and pushed his way into the bunkhouse.

The three of them were standing when he came in, waiting in silence, expressionless. They watched him expectantly as he strode past them to toss his war bag into an empty bunk and wheeled to look at them again. He eased himself down on the bunk and lifted his left leg to tug at his boot. He stopped his action and looked up as Farnell asked: "Where was you when the shootin' started?"

"Looking around," Coppers said easily.

"Find anything?"

Coppers shook his head. "No. Did you?"

"We chased somebody off, maybe two, three. Don't know who but whoever they were they got no business on Slash B land."

Dakota suddenly giggled and Farnell silenced him with a quick hard look and a shake of his head. Farnell swung his head to stare at Coppers: "Just what the hell you doin' here?"

"Riding through," Coppers said, "or maybe staying on if I like it."

"You won't like it," Farnell declared. "I get a funny feeling about you, fella. Just what the hell brings you to this ranch at this time?"

"You ask that of all who come here?" Coppers said, his voice mild.

Farnell's face darkened and his lips stretched thin. "Maybe you better answer questions instead of asking them."

"It's a free country." Dakota's voice caused them all to look at the old man. "A man can come and go free and loose as the wind itself long as he don't bother nobody else, right, Lute?"

"Wrong," Lute said. "We spend a helluva lot of time protecting Slash B property. We ain't got time to chase down saddle tramps and find out what they're up to."

"Who do you have to protect the Slash B from?" Coppers asked, his voice still mild and even.

"Squatters, rustlers, you name them we got 'em."

"To hell with this," Slim said. "I'm goin' to bed." He began unbuttoning his shirt.

"Hold it, Slim," Farnell ordered. "We better take one more look around and see everything is all right."

Farnell walked to the door and jerked it open while Slim rebuttoned his shirt in silence. Slim walked to stand behind Farnell and Dakota took a step toward them to join them.

"I'll spare your old bones," Farnell said. "You stay put, Dakota."

"Sho', boss," Dakota drawled.

Farnell jerked his head and went out with Slim following. The door closed.

Dakota got to his bunk, rummaged around, and then went to the reflectored oil lamp hanging on the wall and adjusted the wick, making the room somewhat brighter. He returned to his bunk, reached under his blankets and brought out a greasy, creased deck of cards, sat down and began laying them out.

"Is Farnell really trying to save your old bones?" Coppers asked.

Dakota grinned. "You don't miss much," he said, shaking his head. "Yeah, Lute is the most hooman of straw bosses I ever worked for. Alluz lookin' out fer ol' folks and leetle kids."

"What's the lay here, Dakota?" Coppers asked. "I mean I get the feeling that all's not well between you and Slim and Farnell."

Dakota simulated surprise. He answered, dropping the half-idiotic tone that seemed to annoy Farnell. "Don't get you, young fella," he said.

"The hell you don't," Coppers answered. "And Farnell—what's his game? Seems I've seen him somewhere—"

"He got here just like you, boy," Dakota said, "one jump ahead o' the law."

Coppers' battered face went wry. "You think that, huh?"

"Yep. Now, didn't you?" He saw Coppers' hesitation and he went on: "Hell, man, you got nothin' to be afraid of here. We're all—" He shut his mouth firmly and squinted up at Coppers. "Maybe I do talk too much."

Coppers got his blankets out of the war bag, spread them on the bunk, and made ready for bed. He sat on the bunk and tugged off the worn boots Gage had left for him in the hotel room in Cheyenne, thinking with a sudden feeling of poignant sadness of his friend. He dropped a boot to the floor and began working on the other one. "Guess I'll be stayin' on, after all," Coppers said.

Dakota continued with his game of solitaire but a chuckle escaped him now and then. Finally, as Coppers prepared to climb into his bunk, he said, "I guessed you would, fella. I figgered you right, didn't I?" His voice held a wistful note.

He's dreaming of his youth, Coppers thought, with some pity. He covered his empathy with a prodigious yawn. "Turn out the light when you're through," he requested and wormed his way down into his blankets.

Coppers was near sleep when Farnell and Slim returned to the bunkhouse. They entered noisily and Coppers came alert at once, shedding his drowsiness.

"I told that saddle tramp to make tracks out of here," Farnell said.

"No you din't, Lute," Dakota said. "Y' jes hinted it."

"We'll settle this in the morning. Let's get some sleep."

Coppers breathed a silent sigh of relief. He had no fear of Farnell. He'd tangled with tougher men and he'd have more of the same in the future. He had confidence in his skill with a gun, and all the years of his life had made him a capable and ready man in dangerous situations.

He was irritated that he couldn't meet Farnell as his natural self, but there was another side to him that allowed him to play roles which were demanded of him at certain times.

When the bunkhouse was quiet, Coppers fell asleep.

CHAPTER TEN

Coppers came awake suddenly in the dark and wondered for a moment where he was. He lay still, listening. Then he heard the floor creaking and the rustling of clothing, the scrape of boots on the floor. Two dark forms moved toward the door. It opened quietly and Coppers knew that Farnell and Slim had prearranged this early-hour departure because not one word had been spoken.

He slept again fitfully and awakened at false dawn. He dressed quietly, hearing Dakota's gusty snores from an adjoining bunk. The old outlaw lay with his head back and mouth open, an unlovely sight but especially so at this early hour.

Outside, Coppers stretched, swelled his chest with an intake of the exhilarating thin air of the altitude; and looked in appreciation at the morning colors of pink and rose and gray rising beyond the swell of the foothills barring his view of the vast plains looking from the west. A streak of yellow sweeping down from near the crest of the foothill was, he knew, a blooming of sunflowers, growing wild and thick in the protection of the shoulder of rocky buttes. A new day and a good one.

Walking slowly back and forth, Coppers concentrated on the east side of the shallow arroyo, scanning the ground carefully. He was halfway up the arroyo when he stopped and rolled a cigarette. He lit it and moodily smoked it down to a stub before he moved on, more slowly now, because he sensed he was close to the scene of the action the night before.

A glitter of brass caught his eye. He squatted and lifted the empty shell case, looking at the cap end. A .38-.40, he read, called by some a .38 Special. Lots of powder behind the .38-caliber bullet. Some men used them because the shells were interchangeable with handgun and rifle. He'd considered that option himself before abandoning it for the stopped capacity of the .44 Colt. His saddle gun was a Winchester 74, using .30-.30 ammunition.

Coppers jammed the empty in his pants pocket, somehow provoked with himself. Why should he scout this ground when he knew almost for certain that Farnell had set up this little action for some purpose known only to himself?

The sun edged over the rounded humps of earth and stone, and the growing heat reached him as he walked across the arroyo to the other side of the shallow valley leading out of the bowl in which the Slash B headquarters were located. He found three spent .41-caliber shells, frowning as he lifted them from the rocky ground, inspecting them and dropping them into the pocket of his brush jacket. Dakota packed a .41 Colt, he was sure; not a rare gun but not as popular as the .44 or .45 Colt. Coppers turned abruptly downhill, walking faster, emerged from the arroyo and saw Dakota trudging toward the castle, leading his saddled horse. Coppers stopped and, realizing he'd not been seen, stepped into the cover of a clump of gray-green sage and a lone pine and watched, his eyes squinted against the glare of the sun.

Dakota stopped before the kitchen door and Wash came out, gave him a package, and spoke a few words before turning back into the castle. Dakota stowed the package in his saddlebags, buckled the straps, mounted and trotted his horse toward the road leading to town.

Coppers stepped out from his cover and moved to intercept the old man, throwing up his hand.

"Howdy," Dakota said, reining in, looking at him curiously. "You're out early fer a guy ridin' the grubline." His look was cool and slightly contemptuous, the effects, Coppers realized, of his effort to placate Farnell the night before.

"It's a habit I can't get rid of," Coppers said.

"Yeah. Bad things to get inter. Habits, I mean."

"Maybe. You riding into town?"

"Sho' nuff. Need anythin'?"

Coppers shook his head. "I need a lot but can't afford much."

Dakota didn't smile. "I know whatcha mean." He lifted his reins. "It's gonna be a long day."

"You go in every day?" Coppers asked curiously.

"Nope. Just when needful, like today. The old man is sending another batch to Denver."

Coppers felt his heartbeat quicken but his face remained impassive. "Batch?"

"Yeah. The ol' duck is writing his mem—memwars, I guess you call 'em. When he gets some done he sends them to this word perfesser over Denver way."

Coppers watched Dakota out of sight, over the swell of a rounded hill of green and gray that would turn brown before too much time passed. When Dakota's hat bobbed below the rim of land, Coppers went to the barn and put the sorry saddle on the buckskin. He mounted in the barn and rode out through the wide double doors, ducking his head to avoid the overhead beam. He hauled the horse in sharply to avoid Aletha.

She stood there looking up at him. It startled him for a moment because it seemed that she could *see* him.

She said nothing at first and he watched her, noticing the curve of her body and the gleam of her hair. She moved her head and spoke to him with some strange restraint in her voice.

"I was hoping you'd stay."

"I don't know if I'd be much use to you."

"Let me be the judge of that. I want you to stay." She came closer to him, reached out her hand and stroked Bucky's muzzle. She was near enough for him to lean down and touch her; and he wanted to do it, for her closeness unloosed something in him that was sharp and biting, almost painful. It was a feeling suddenly blossoming that made him want to run and he'd never in his life run from anything.

He touched Bucky with his spurs but held the reins tight. She felt the movement of the horse and stepped back quickly, resignation on her face. Her voice held a note of gloom. "You are in a hurry to leave. I'm sorry."

"You can't be in any danger here," he said, more to quiet his own fears. "That shooting last night—" He was about to tell her that the raid was a fake, staged by Farnell, but he stopped short, thinking that he should tell that to Farnell in a showdown that was sure to come.

"It's not the first time," she said simply. "The worst one happened just after we got here. We went to Mr. Bennion's Box MB for a housewarming and barn-raising—his new venture. When we returned home the next day our house had been ransacked, everything torn up, as though someone was searching for something."

He thought about that so long that she tilted her head and said, "You understand what I said, Dave?"

"Yes." He found it difficult to speak as he meant to without causing her undue alarm. "I've got to leave. But I'll be back. I promise."

She smiled then, the soft curve of her lips unbearably beautiful. "I'll be looking for you," she said in a soft voice.

Coppers remembered the sound of her voice and all of her words as he put Bucky into a run so as to not allow Dakota too much of a head start on him. What he planned depended on reaching town just a short time after Dakota arrived there.

He kept to the main road as it went up and down and around, following the original contours made first by buffalo and then range cattle, gradually swinging in closer to the mountains bulking in the west. The road took him past small and large hill-enclosed valleys with belly-deep grass curing to a lush brown in the oncoming summer sun. He shook his head in disgust at the waste. That grass would fatten many cattle and he was pained to see it going unused.

He kept a careful watch so as not to let Dakota know he was being followed. As yet he hadn't caught sight of the old outlaw, but there was a faint smell of dust in the air and he knew Dakota was not too far ahead.

Far away he heard a bell tolling, a distant sound. Riding on, he listened, deciding it was a call to the town's school kids. His shadow rode beside him, considerably shortened from when he'd started his ride earlier. He slowed Bucky to a walk when he caught sight of dust ahead. The road curved and climbed, entered a saddle with hills bulking on either side. A moment later he looked down into the town of Arapaho.

He dismounted and led the horse off the road. He stopped in a cluster of pine trees and loosened Bucky's cinch, stroked the sweaty neck, and watched Dakota enter the town on his long-barreled chestnut, still loping. Even as Coppers watched, he saw

Dakota, slumping in the saddle, stop his horse in the middle of the wide dusty street. Dakota looked first at the false-fronted building with a façade sign stating that herein was the U. S. POST OFFICE. Then he deliberately turned his head to look at another false front labeled the Wild Belle Saloon. In the clear air Dakota's shrugged shoulders were plainly visible. The old outlaw urged his horse toward the post office. Duty had won over pleasure. Coppers sat on the ground, his elbows on his knees, holding Bucky's reins, while the horse nibbled at a few blades of brown grass.

Dakota tied in at the rail while his horse drank from the leaky wooden trough at the end of the rack. As Coppers watched, Dakota unbuckled his saddlebags and removed the package. He tucked it under his arm while he redid the straps of his saddlebags. He bowlegged his way toward the post office, his spurs raising tendrils of dust, crossed the wooden walk, mounted the steps, and disappeared inside the building which also bore a striped barber's pole beside the door.

Not more than five minutes after Dakota entered the post office, Coppers heard the sounds of an approaching rider. He got to his feet, gathered the reins, and led Bucky farther away from the road and into a pine copse, out of sight of the road, yet able to see through the branches. He held his hand loosely over Bucky's muzzle and placed his other hand against the gelding's belly to sense a swell of the barrel and the beginning of a neigh. Bucky looked at him curiously and pumped his head. The horseman, a cowboy from his appearance, loped past without noticing Coppers hidden in the second-growth pine.

When the sounds of the passerby died, Coppers returned to his original spot and looked down into the town, unprepossessing, slumbrous, not much activity. A double row of buildings lined either side of the road and other buildings were scattered around in the bright sunshine, including a white steeple-topped building which Coppers guessed doubled as church and school. A few horses, either picketed or hobbled, grazed near the building. A plank bridge spanned the creek between Coppers and the town. Most of the buildings were unpainted, single story, squatting side by side. Another road, coming down from the higher hills, formed an intersection. On the four corners thus formed stood a hotel, a general store, and two saloons facing each other, one the Wild Belle Saloon and the other simply labeled as Saloon. Beyond the Saloon was a livery stable and a blacksmith shop. He looked for and found the marshal's shack where he'd taken the body of Gil Tatum, which he'd turned over to ancient old Al Hunter, the deputy.

Coppers had his look and got out the makings, rolling up a cigarette which he lighted, sticking the spent match into the dirt between his feet. He didn't really want a cigarette but it served to give him something to do for the moment.

Coppers caught a sudden movement at the door of the post office. Dakota emerged, empty-handed now, and without hesitation struck out across the street toward the Wild Belle and disappeared within the swinging doors. Coppers could imagine Dakota having a drink, perhaps a cold beer, and he felt saliva form in his mouth. Hours later, as the sun began to drop below the horizon, Coppers stiffened as he saw Dakota emerge from the Wild Belle and weave his way toward his horse, stumbling. Dakota had trouble mounting but finally made it up only to find his horse still tied to the hitch rack. He slumped in his saddle as three men stopped before Dakota and spoke. Coppers could only guess what was being said as the old man weaved in his saddle. One man held the bridle of Dakota's horse and the other two came up beside Dakota and one of them reached up and yanked Dakota out of the saddle and let him fall on the ground.

A small group had begun to gather in the quickening twilight but none interfered as Dakota was pulled to his feet and dragged into the alley between the post office and a saddle shop.

Coppers went to his horse, mounted, and put Bucky back to the road. Once on the road he urged the horse into a hard run down the winding road into Arapaho. He thundered over the bridge and almost ran over a man crossing the street. The man yelled a frightened curse as he leaped out of the way.

Coppers came up beside Dakota's horse and dismounted. A small cluster of men were grouped around the mouth of the alley and Coppers went through them, ignoring their protests. The sound of blows, grunts, and curses came to him as he entered the alley. The dark shapes in the gloom of early evening were barely visible as he grabbed the man kneeling over Dakota, pounding at him with something held in his fist. He slammed the man against the side of the building as the other two hit out at Coppers. He backed away, drawing his pistol, and the three of them ran, pounding down the alley. Coppers had never fired his pistol at a retreating man and he did not do so now, though the urge was high.

At the appearance of the gun, the small group at the mouth of the alley silently dispersed. Coppers approached Dakota, kneeling above him, smelling the strong odor of whiskey rising from the old man. Holstering his pistol, Coppers struck a match, holding it over Dakota, to see a battered and bloody face. They'd done a good job wrecking the old man in a very short space of time.

Coppers pulled him upright, into a sitting position. Dakota mumbled something Coppers couldn't understand. He lifted the old man easily, put him across his shoulder, and headed down the street toward the livery stable.

There was no one about the stable. He placed Dakota on the ground against the front of the building and went inside, taking the lantern from a nail beside the door. He found a clean stall. He came back to Dakota, lifted him and took him down the odorous runway to the stall he'd selected and put him on a pile of clean straw. He placed bars across the stall, hung the lantern back on its hook, and returned to the street, moving swiftly, filled with a sense of urgency, of being pulled in many directions at the same time.

He crossed the wooden walk and entered the post office. A tall, thin bald man was filling a lamp with coal oil as Coppers stood inside the door. The man nodded at Coppers and went on with his task. When the oil reservoir was full, he placed his oil can on the floor, stabbed a piece of potato over the pouring spout, replaced the wick in the oil reservoir, screwed it down and lighted it; he replaced the lamp chimney and turned to Coppers, wiping his hands on the long white apron that reached to his knees. The post office was also a barbershop and contained a supply of patent medicines on the shelf. A sign on the wall stated that Albert Dexter, the prop. also pulled teeth.

"What'll it be, stranger, a bottle of Hotstetter's? A shave and a haircut? Aching tooth, maybe?"

"None of those," Coppers said. "I'm a new hand at the Slash B, Mr. Dexter. Mr. Boynton sent me in. He wasn't sure he addressed that package to Denver correctly. The package Dakota brought in. Mr. Boynton wanted me to check it and make sure it was right."

Albert Dexter blinked at Coppers. "I recollect it was writ same as the others."

"Your recollect isn't good enough," Coppers said, not quite as easy now. "I'll look at it to make sure."

"Well, now, I don't know—" He stopped speaking on seeing the iciness in Coppers' eyes and something more than that which he couldn't identify. The feeling he easily recognized as fear, from the coldness entering his belly and weakening his knees, decided him. He hated himself for giving in so quickly, but all of a sudden this big man seemed so menacing. "I'll get it for you," he said quickly, "even if it's awready in the mail sack. But the stage won't come till tomorrow, so it don't make no difference."

"I appreciate that," Coppers said, not relaxing.

"No trouble at all," the man said, hastening to the portion of the building devoted to handling the mail. There was a wicket in the counter and a rack of pigeonholes nailed to the wall behind the wicket, some of them containing letters. Mr. Dexter continued nervously: "I always try to accommodate people who come in here for one thing or another. Ah, here 'tis."

He brought the package, scanning it as he walked to stand before Coppers. He passed the package to Coppers. "See, just like I said. Same as all the others."

Coppers took the package and looked at the address. It was penned in graceful script to Lemuel P. Taylor, Esq., Windsor Hotel, Denver, Colorado.

"So it is," Coppers said, returning the package to Dexter. He turned away and on second thought wheeled back to Dexter who stood attentively before him. "Is there a telegraph office in town, Mr. Dexter?"

"No, sir, sure ain't. Not as such. We built one when we thought the railroad was comin' through. But they didn't give us even a spur and we never did get to use it."

"I suppose the nearest telegraph is in Laramie?"

"No, there's one at Muddy Creek. Whoa up; Muddy Creek is

nothin' but loadin' pens and a lil dinky station, an' the only time there's a telegraph operator there is when cattle is bein' shipped."

The talky Mr. Dexter didn't seem about to run down. Coppers said, "Thanks," and turned toward the door.

"But you can get a message out, though," Mr. Dexter called, as though anxious to detain a possible customer. "That feller what owns the Box MB has got hisself a telephone for all them dudes. He's got a dude ranch, you know. First one in these parts."

"Thank you, Mr. Dexter," Coppers said from the door.

"You welcome. Sure you don't want somethin'? That Hotstetter's is good for just about anything—" He stopped speaking when he realized Coppers was no longer there.

CHAPTER ELEVEN

Standing in the darkness on the edge of the wooden walk a few doors down from the post office, Coppers looked at the town while he considered his next move. A group of three horsemen rode slowly through town, entered the alley between the Wild Belle and the building next to it, and he wondered who they were, from whence they came, and where they were going. A few lighted houses displayed yellow rectangles of light in some windows. Many others were dark.

While he looked over this rough town, he considered his next move. He'd found a name in Denver. Lemuel P. Taylor, and don't forget the Esq., he told himself. This man could be helping Boynton with his memoirs—he could be helping him deal stolen and bogus money. The problem of getting word to the Denver agent involved his sending a coded message to that worthy, requesting an S & R—agency shorthand for Surveillance and Report. He had to be about it quickly.

Coppers had no doubt of his ability to gain entrance to the closed station at Muddy Creek, where he could make use of the telegraph line. He had the expertise to do it; he'd been fascinated by the Morse code early on. During the long dawdling voyage to Cuba, an expert Morse operator had taught him the code. By doing it himself he'd save many miles of travel and more hours of time than he could afford.

First things first, he told himself, and strode off into the night to check on the livery stable and Dakota.

He stooped and crawled under the bar he'd placed across the stall and struck a match. Dakota was as he'd left him. The old man would probably sleep the night away. He seemed to be breathing easily and only groaned and ground his teeth as Coppers pulled him into a more comfortable position.

Walking back to his horse, Coppers stopped at the watering trough and splashed cold water on his face. Cool currents flowing down the mountain chilled his skin and dried the droplets of water on his face. Music came from the Wild Belle as the town began coming alive. The town took on a different character at night, no longer appearing a dead or dying entity.

After watering his horse, Coppers mounted and headed out southwest, toward the Muddy Creek siding. He quelled his impatience, knowing that there were certain events in the future he could not control because he was not aware of them.

As he rode, the moon came out and laid a yellow patina on the land. The brightness of the moon put his shadow, short and grotesque, beside him on the trail. He came presently to where the faint traces of a wagon road branched off, the twin ruts meandering over an adjacent ridge. He paused only a moment to get his bearing and then kept to the more plainly marked road.

By degrees the land flattened and the tangy odor of scrub pine was replaced by stronger-smelling sage. He stopped once, thinking he'd heard a sound. He sat silently, listening for a repetition of the sound, and heard nothing except the squeak of leather and the clack of a bit as Bucky shook his head. He rode on, holding Bucky to a slow walk, listening. He heard the sound again as he felt Bucky's muscles bunch as the horse picked its way down into a dry wash. He distinctly heard the sound an ironshod hoof makes striking a rock. He headed Bucky up the dry wash and rode a hundred feet off the trail and dismounted, tying the horse to the roots of an old stump that had floated down in some past cloudburst. Bending, he removed his spurs and stuck them through the loops of buckskin that held his saddle together. Then he went back along the rock-strewn wash and squatted behind a clump of sage, watching the road.

The two riders stopped on the edge of the dry wash. Only their heads and shoulders were visible and the tips of their horses' ears. They had been talking but they stopped when their horses stopped, sitting silently, listening.

"I ain't goin' another damn step, Spud," one of the men said in a loud voice.

"All right, all right," Spud answered. "We just gotta make certain, that's all. I don't like it any better than the next one, ridin' all over hell 'n gone on a wild-goose chase."

"Then let's turn around and head back. He's probably another one of them on the run, headin' for Brown's Hole, or Star Valley. The old Laramie Road ends up in Star, at the south end."

"I know that."

"We gonna sit here all night?"

"All right, then, let's turn around and hightail it."

The men disappeared from sight and the sound of their passing slowly died away to nothing. Coppers heard the whir of wings as some night hunting bird winged away. In the far distance a coyote barked sharply.

Coppers walked back to his horse, who whickered a welcome. He put his spurs in his saddlebags, rubbed Bucky's sweaty neck, and, mounting, headed back to the road. On reaching the road, Coppers turned Bucky toward Muddy Creek, resisting an urge to follow the two men. He had an idea that he'd meet them again— if they were Lute Farnell's hired hands.

Even at a distance, in the quiet of the night, he could hear the tinny clack of the telegraph sounder. He passed the empty stock pens with the lingering smell of cattle still hanging in the air. Dismounting, Coppers loosened the cinch, ran his hand under the damp saddle blanket, smoothing the sweaty hair. He led Bucky into one of the near pens and closed the gate. The horse followed him along the fence as Coppers walked toward the building bulking in the night. Twin rails of silver went off into the distance to be lost in the curve of the hills.

Coppers walked around the building, which was almost square and sat on a platform close to the rails, the mainline, and siding that held cars when cattle were being loaded; now, it was empty. Attached to the depot was a small lean-to, which held, Coppers guessed, a handcar and tools for gandy dancers, and workers who kept the track in repair. Down the tracks, a quarter of a mile away, he could make out a water tank for steam engines.

Coppers tried all the windows and the door and found them locked. All the while, he was listening to the chatter of the telegraph sounder inside the building, getting a sense of what was going on along the wire, which was on the mainline from San Francisco to Denver, with all stations in between hooked in. As a matter of fact there was more than one wire—one being reserved for Western Union business and the other handling only railroad traffic. Coppers was interested in the message traffic on the WU wire, and by the time he'd used his knife to pop a latch on one of the windows, he knew the call signs of operators at each end of the wire. He listened intently, trying to identify the outstanding characteristic touch of each telegraph operator, meaning to imitate the style when he was ready to put his own messages on the wire.

Inside the building he stood still, orienting himself. The bright moonlight outside filtered into the interior of the frame building, making objects plainly visible. A musty odor, hanging in the air, attested abandonment. The Muddy Creek station opened only to accommodate large shipments of cattle, for the convenience of buyers, commission agents, and shippers.

Walking across the room, he identified the plugs of the switching arrangements. He got the code book from between the lining of his battered boots, feeling a twinge of grief as he realized Harlan Gage had placed it there and perhaps that was one of his last acts. He composed messages, one to the Denver operative and another to Effington (all official messages went to Effington), in Washington, D.C., addressed to a preplanted drop number on an obscure residential street. When all was ready, he cut the wire with a switch during a lull in the telegraph chatter. He took up the rhythm and was busy acting as a relay station. He'd copy a message from San Francisco and relay it to Denver and also reverse it, relaying between Denver and San Francisco. At last an inconsequential message came through, which he discarded, putting the number of the discarded message on his own telegram. He transmitted both messages and afterward continued to relay messages back and forth. When there was another lull in telegrams, he switched the line back to normal. He crawled through the window and closed it behind him. After letting Bucky drink, he turned the horse toward Arapaho, going at a steady mile-eating lope, resisting an urge to doze in the saddle.

The stars were gone, and rose and gold colors formed behind the gray dawning when Coppers rode into the sleeping town. He was bone-tired and irritable when he dismounted outside the livery stable. Dakota lay with his head back, his mouth open, his hands clenched and resting on his chest, twitching now and then in his sleep. Leaning over, Coppers shook Dakota roughly. "Come on, old man, let's get moving."

Dakota blubbered and tried to roll on his side. Coppers pulled him upright and heaved him to his feet. He guided Dakota to his horse and got him in the saddle.

"You're a mess, old man," Coppers muttered as he mounted Bucky and took the reins of Dakota's horse and led the animal down the street. Dakota swayed in the saddle, his eyes clenched shut, both hands gripping the saddle horn.

Their horses thumped across the bridge and began the climb toward the higher hills. They reached the top and Coppers stopped to let the horses blow.

"Wha' y' stoppin'?" Dakota asked hoarsely.

"To rest the horses," Coppers snapped. "Why were those fellows beating on you, Dakota?"

"I got drunk," Dakota said. "I don't remember much when I get soused like that."

"Do you know them? They local people?"

"Hell, no, never laid eyes on 'em before. Country's fillin' up with shady characters." He clutched his belly with both hands, groaning. "Ol' Al Hunter, best depitty in the county, shot down like a dog night 'er so ago. Never had no truck with lawmen but Al was a real fine man." He groaned again, leaning over to retch but nothing came up.

Coppers was staring at Dakota. "Al Hunter, did you say? When did this happen?"

"Same night some yahoo brought in the body of a dude wrangler named Gil Tatum. Somebody shot ol' Al in the back."

Coppers had an eerie feeling suddenly come on him that Gil Tatum and Al Hunter may have been killed by the same murderer. And maybe, just maybe, he told himself, I might be involved. A trail of dead men began on his back trail from the moment he stepped off the train in Cheyenne. He mounted his horse and headed to the road.

Dakota followed. "Thanks," he said.

"For what?"

"Helpin' me out like you did."

"If you know I helped you, you must know something else. What did they say while they were pounding you into a chunk of liver?"

"They asked me somethin' like where's the money hid? I don't know nothin' about no money. Never heard tell anythin' 'bout it, either."

They rode on in silence for a few minutes and then Dakota spoke again: "I hate to tell you this but I gotta do it. Lute told me to tell you to make tracks outta here. Said they ain't no job for you now or later on, no matter what Miss Aletha says."

Coppers was silent.

Dakota persisted. "Ain't you gonna say nothin'? Lute's a dangerous man and Slim is twice as nasty. Slim'll shoot you in the back if'n he can't get you any other way. My advice is go while you got a chance."

"Thanks, Dakota," Coppers said quietly. "I appreciate your worry on my account."

CHAPTER TWELVE

It was near noon when Coppers and Dakota rode into the Slash B ranch. They cared for their horses in silence and afterward Dakota stumbled toward the bunkhouse.

"I'm gonna sleep till Lute comes and wakes me up," he called over his shoulder.

"When'll that be?"

Dakota didn't slow as he answered, "Dunno. Don't care either." He disappeared into the bunkhouse and slammed the door shut.

Coppers watched as both horses rolled in the dust of the corral then got up shaking themselves.

A motion drew his eyes to the castle. Aletha Boynton came out the front door, crossed the porch, and came with a firm step upon the ground and stood for a moment.

Coppers kept his eyes on her as she positioned herself and, turning slightly away from him and then directly at him, walked forward with a pleased smile on her smooth and lovely face.

"We're going to the Box MB, remember?" she asked.

He felt tired but his irritability disappeared when he caught sight of her. A ride to Bennion's ranch didn't seem desirable right at that time but he knew he'd not refuse her. "When you're ready," he said. "My horse is all used up, though."

"Take any horse in the small pasture," she said. "Saddle the blaze-faced sorrel with the front-left white stocking for me." She blushed faintly.

He smiled slightly. "Fine. What about Farah?"

"Can't we lead her?"

"Sure. I'll get everything ready."

She turned her head away. "I'm so glad you're back, Dave."

"I'm glad to be back," he said, and stood waiting as she moved away from him. When she disappeared into the castle, he got his rope from his saddle and walked to the small pasture, leaning on the bars, looking at the half-dozen horses inside the pole enclosure. All of them stopped feeding and looked back at him, heads raised, ears erect, bright-eyed and watchful.

They were better horses than those usually found on a working ranch, big and strong and shiny slick, indicating they were not only grain-fed but well groomed. Crawling through the bars as the horses clustered for protection against the rope, Coppers shook out a small loop and flipped it toward the blaze-faced sorrel. The rope landed across the ears of the snorting horse, and with a flip of the wrist, he settled the rope around the glossy neck. He went hand over hand down the rope, scattering the herd, and took a halter turn around the mouth of the horse with his rope and led the animal outside the corral and tied it to a snubbing post near the barn door. He found the sidesaddle in the tack room and carried it outside where he slapped it on the sorrel and cinched it down tight. He roped a big bay for himself and got it ready for riding. When that was done, he brought Farah from her stall in the barn, fastened a lead rope to the hackamore and looped it around his saddle horn.

When Aletha emerged from the castle in her riding habit, Coppers was leaning against his horse, waiting. He helped her to mount and watched while she settled herself. When she nodded her readiness, Coppers stepped into his own saddle. The bay bucked a few short jumps and then decided to give it up.

The two horses walked side by side in the twin ruts as the road looped back and forth between the hills. Far off to the left, to the west, Coppers could see the gray upthrust of sharp-pointed granite peaks, bright in the sunshine. He described to her the formation of cumulus over the mountains, towering white cauliflower-like heads, which, driven by the wind, became sheep's backs, drifting over the valley, laying dark shadows on the land. While he talked, he watched the motion of her rounded body move with the motion of her horse.

Not knowing how to bring up the subject, he blurted: "Do you ever want to leave here, go back East?"

Surprise washed over her face as she turned toward him.

"What an idea! No, no, Dave, I love it here. I'd rather be here than anywhere else in the whole world."

"Your grandfather is old," Coppers said bluntly. "What'll you do when he's gone? It's something you'll have to face one day."

Her face darkened slightly as she frowned. "You've changed your mind?"

He looked at her blankly and then realized he must put his answer in words. "Have I changed my mind about what?"

"You accepted the fact that I get along very well," she said, a dry edge in her voice. "For a blind person? I had assumed you meant I could make my way as well as a sighted one."

"I didn't mean it that way," he protested, an uneasiness unsettling him. "I mean—oh, the devil I don't know what I mean."

She laughed and leaned over to squeeze his hand.

The road they followed joined another, more heavily traveled. A short time later this new road rose with the land and they topped a long low ridge. Coppers whistled softly, stopping his horse. Aletha's horse stopped and she turned a questioning look on him.

"We're at the top of a high, rocky, pine-covered ridge," Coppers said. "The road drops right down to the Box MB." He surveyed the extensive buildings and corral. "I had no idea Bennion had such a big place."

There were two sizable barns, one larger than the other; a large circular corral that filled the area between cabins along the creek and the barns; and a holding pen and smaller buildings that housed a blacksmith shop, a smoke and ice house, and quarters for the crew.

Along the bank of the creek, among the pine and spruce, was a long line of what Coppers imagined to be guest cabins. A footbridge spanned the creek leading to the main ranch house, which stood in solitary splendor among towering flickering-leaved aspens. The main ranch, a hip-roofed building with a porch running around three sides, also boasted a stone chimney. Two or three other more pretentious lodges were scattered in the spruce and pine along the far side of the creek.

Coppers counted eleven horses in the round corral. He didn't bother to count those in the pasture but he estimated that there must be a total of at least forty head of riding stock in sight. He whistled softly.

"Mr. Bennion has invested quite a bit in this place," Aletha said. "He's a hard worker."

"That's plain to see," Coppers said. "Let's ride on down."

They left the road above the ranch house and followed a horse trail through the pines. A dog came from somewhere barking a welcome.

Circling the house, Coppers dismounted and helped Aletha to the ground as Sal Bennion came out on the porch, holding the baby on her hip, shading her eyes from the westering sun as she stood on the top step, smiling her pleasure. Her eyes went to Coppers and she gave a start of recognition and her smile faded.

"Come—come on in the house, Aletha," Sal invited, struggling to regain her composure.

"Sal, how nice to visit you again."

"Let me take your arm," Aletha whispered to Coppers, low-voiced. "I'm not sure of myself here."

Obediently, Coppers took her hand and brought it to his arm and started up the steps. She kept close to him and he breathed deeply of her sweet fragrance. At the top step she left him, going forward, leaning to kiss Sal's cheek.

Still looking at Coppers with frightened eyes, Sal said, "I'll put the baby down, then we'll have coffee. Or tea, if you'd like that better."

"Let me hold the baby a minute," Aletha begged, and took the baby from Sal, who led her to a wood and leather couch that stood against the wall.

With the baby on her lap, Aletha laughed gaily and talked to the wide-eyed, interested child.

"You don't mind if I look around?" Coppers asked. "We did bring Farah over for your vet to take a look at her."

Sal nodded dumbly, apparently not hearing his words.

"You've got quite a spread here, Mrs. Bennion," Coppers said easily, trying to put the woman at ease.

"Thank you. Mel's so proud of it. He's off on a trail ride with the guests and he'll be back some time later today."

Coppers turned down the steps.

She followed him out into the yard, looking anxiously at him, almost pleadingly.

"Don't be afraid I'm going to spill anything. Not that there's anything worth spilling. But I'd appreciate it if you'd not mention to anyone—not a single person—that you've ever seen me before. We'll have our own secret." He smiled at her and was rewarded with an uncertain smile.

She thinks I'm on the run, Coppers thought, and was satisfied to let it go at that.

"Where'll I find your vet?"

"Doc Jasper? He went out to look at some sick cows this morning, but his horse is in the corral so he's back. He'll be over there in the log house—or nearby." She pointed to a small old log shack near the barn. "He stays there mostly, in the old bunkhouse which he uses now since the crew got new quarters."

He thanked her, touched his hat, and led Farah toward the vet's shack.

A tall, thin man of about sixty, with a shock of white hair peppered with black, stepped out the door, adjusting his wire-rimmed glasses. His white shirt sleeves were rolled up and he wore bright red suspenders to hold up his soiled blue pants, which apparently at one time had been part of a stylish suit. His boots were without spurs. His face was beginning to fall in with age, his jowls sagging, his neck corded and ridged. He nodded at Coppers, looking at the horse.

"Looks like Aletha's mare," he said.

"It is," Coppers said. "I'm Dave, new hired hand at the Slash B," wondering why Bennion hired a full-time vet for his operation.

Coppers explained how Farah got her wounds.

"Seems to be doing all right," Doc Jasper muttered. "May help to put on some healing salve." He straightened, looking at Dave. "I'll go get it."

Jasper entered the log shack and Dave followed, watching the vet paw amid the clutter on a shelf. He brought down a lard can, pried off the lid, and sniffed at it. "Pretty good stuff here; helps fight infection."

Dave lifted his eyes to the sign above the shelf, hand-lettered: Jasper Bartell, D.V.M.

"I thought your last name was Jasper," Dave said.

The vet shook his head. "I been called Doc Jasper since I was a vet student in Kansas," he said. "Most people have forgotten my last name, if they ever knew it."

He walked past Dave, heading for the door, swinging the bucket by its bail.

"Isn't it unusual for a ranch to have a vet all its own?" Dave asked.

Jasper nodded. "Well, yes. You might say I'm here as the result of a rescue mission by Mel Bennion."

"Rescue mission?"

"Yes. Me. I got in a bunch of trouble few years back. Messed up my practice, took to the bottle, and was about to drink myself to death when Mel Bennion brought me out here and got me on my feet. Good man, Mel."

On reaching the restless Farah, Jasper stood looking at her critically. "You better get a good grip on her," he said. "This'll sting her for a minute or two and she's liable to cut up some, get a little snorty."

"You got a twister?" Dave asked.

"Don't use 'em," Jasper said shortly. "Just hang on her upper lip with your fingers; let her know you got her. She won't fight."

Coppers got a firm grip on Farah's hackamore with one hand and with the thumb and forefinger of his right hand grasped the mare's upper lip but didn't squeeze hard. "All right, put it on," he said.

The mare flinched and trembled, her hindquarters sagging as Jasper applied the salve to the wounds. Coppers talked soothingly to the mare and tightened his grip on her nose to let her know she should not try to bolt.

"There, that'll do it," Doc Jasper said, stepping back. "I'll put some of this salve in a smaller container for you to take with you. Keep it on her wounds till they stop draining and she'll be fine. Great mare, this one."

"She is," agreed Coppers.

Coppers and Jasper turned as a long, faraway whoop sounded, and the Box MB stage plunged down the hill toward ranch headquarters.

"That's Humpy Wilcox on the lines," Jasper said with quiet

satisfaction. "Best damn driver in the business, which is too bad because stages are going out of use. That's the old Cheyenne to Deadwood stage, which a bunch of Easterners were about to buy when Mel stepped in and took it away from them. Saving it for its historical value, he said, but I got a good idea he wanted little Mel to see what some of the Old West was like when the kid grows up."

"He runs that stage all the way to Cheyenne and back?"

Jasper shook his head. "Nope. Meets the train in Laramie twice a week, at Laramie depot, and brings a few dudes now and then."

"How many guests are here now?" Coppers asked.

"About thirty. They're all out on a trail ride now. Be back later today and there'll be plenty of work for me to do. The dudes are hard on horses."

Thirty. My God! Coppers thought. The task of checking out thirty pilgrims seemed impossible.

"More than half are women," Jasper continued. "They're quite a bunch, this group. There's a very young and pretty school teacher from Chicago who's causing more trouble than a stampede on a trail drive." He looked at Coppers for his reaction.

Coppers shrugged. There was always something like that in a group of people with a variety of backgrounds.

Coppers saw a movement along the creek and swiveled his head in that direction. A man in waders to his armpits emerged from the trees with a fishing rod in his hand. His hat was well filled with fishing flies.

"Who's that?"

Doc Jasper chuckled wryly. "H. Richard Donel, the most famous newspaperman in the world to hear him tell it." There was plain distaste in the vet's tone.

"Why isn't he on the trail ride? He is a guest, right?"

Jasper shrugged. "Scared of horses, I think. He claims to have an old wound from the Cuba war. I think he got dysentery or something similar."

Donel disappeared from view into a cluster of cottonwood trees along the creek bank. "A tenderfoot afraid of horses vacationing on a dude ranch?" Dave asked incredulously.

"I suspect he's got something up his sleeve. He's looking for veterans who were in Roosevelt's Rough Riders. Way he tells it, Donel swears Teddy recruited all the killers, outlaws, and dirty scum he could find to fight in Cuba. Donel's trying to build a case against Teddy, digging up dirt to discredit our President. That's a pretty damn unpopular cause in these parts."

"It could get him killed," agreed Coppers. "Just what is Donel doing to dig out this information?"

"So far he's talked to some of Bennion's riders. Two of them were in the Spanish-American War, but they served in the Philippines. Guess Donel is looking for men who went with Teddy to Cuba. Come on; we'll turn Farah into the small pasture next to the round corral. Plenty of water and feed in there and she won't be bothered by any other horses."

Coppers untied the lead rope and, leading Farah, followed Doc Jasper to the small corral. Jasper opened the gate and Coppers removed the lead line and waved the mare into the enclosure. He stood for a moment watching Farah race around the small corral.

"I've got to get ready to look at some used-up horses," Doc Jasper said and walked toward his log-cabin office and dispensary.

Coppers waited until Doc Jasper disappeared into his shack and then walked to the nearest footbridge, one of several, and crossed the creek. The cabins on that side of the creek were more pretentious than the ones clustered between the corral and barns and other outbuildings.

Just as Coppers thought, the newsman, Donel, emerged from the trees and walked rapidly toward the cabin nearest the main ranch house.

Coppers raised his hand.

Donel's walk slowed and then he stopped, staring at Coppers. "You're a stranger," he said.

"I work at the Slash B, for the Boyntons."

"The Boyntons? Ah, yes. Is Aletha here?"

Coppers felt a stab of jealousy at Donel's casual use of Aletha's name. He nodded. "She's visiting with Mrs. Bennion." He studied Donel covertly, not impressed with what he saw. "Doc Jasper tells me you're interested in interviewing Cuban veterans who served with Roosevelt."

Donel's face tightened and he nodded. "Yes, that's true."

"Why look out in a remote place like this? Why not in Cheyenne or Denver, or at least where you'd have more people to talk to?"

"I have my reasons for being here," Donel said stiffly. "Those reasons are good enough for me, for the time being."

"What have you found out?"

"I've found all I need to know. What I'm looking for now is documentation—proof if you will."

"Proof of what?"

"You're not a newsman, are you?" Donel asked, in a tone of suspicion, suddenly cautious.

Coppers laughed, gesturing with his hands to his sorry outfit. "Do I look like a newsman?"

"Your outward appearance says no," Donel said evenly, "but there's something about you that says something else. Were you in the Rough Riders? Is that where you got all those scars?"

Coppers didn't hesitate to lie. "No, I'm just what I seem to be, a wandering cowpoke." Coppers had met few men who made direct reference to his scarred face. Meeting for the first time, some would stare and avert their eyes. Others stared and continued to stare. But few voiced the question Donel had made so easily and without a thought that it might have been improper. His initial dislike of Donel deepened.

Donel grunted. "You're just as well off," he said. "Being a member of that band of cutthroat killers is no honor, no indeed!"

"I'm afraid you have the wrong information," Coppers said coldly. "I had friends among them. I know what they are."

"Indeed? Well, fellow, let me tell you this: I was there in person and I got to know them well. The biggest bunch of outlaws, murderers, and killers ever assembled together in the history of wars. And, believe me, Roosevelt knew what they were. He actively recruited this type, knowing most of them were wanted by the law."

"Nonsense! Roosevelt is held in very high esteem around the country and particularly in the West."

"Hah! I'll personally explode the Roosevelt myth and, believe me, I have the wherewith to do it."

Coppers felt his self-control crumpling even while he told himself it'd be utter foolishness to get into a fight with this pip-squeak of a newsman. He muttered, "Sorry I can't wish you luck. No, I take that back. I'm not sorry." He turned from Donel, feeling the urge to knock the man down but resisting.

The leading rider from the Box MB trail ride emerged from the pine trees at the southwest edge of the ranch proper and began descending into the valley. Soon a long serpentine line of horses and riders, raising a cloud of dust, wound down the gently sloping hills. Even at this distance they appeared bedraggled and worn.

Coppers crossed another footbridge farther down and strode to Doc Jasper's log shack. The door was open and inside he could see Jasper puttering around with a Bunsen burner which he abandoned as Coppers leaned the point of his shoulder against the door frame.

"See them yet?" Jasper asked.

Coppers nodded. "They'll be here in twenty minutes the rate they're riding."

Doc Jasper came to the door, and Coppers swung around to see a rider, sitting tall in the saddle of an uncommonly big calico, ride out of the coulee far ahead of the column's lead rider. Coppers had seen Mel Bennion only once, briefly, that night at the Cheyenne depot, but he recognized the rancher at once.

"There's Mel now," Jasper said. "At the end of a trail ride Mel can't wait to get away from the dudes. Can't stand 'em."

As Bennion neared his house, the old Cheyenne-Deadwood stage came rocketing down the hill at a full gallop, the four horses stretched out, manes and tails flying, with Humpy Wilcox yippeeing like crazy and popping his whip.

"Is he crazy?" Coppers muttered.

"That's the way old Humpy ends his trip," Jasper said, as the stage hit the creek and raised a great silver sheet of water.

This scene was imprinted in Coppers' mind and then something was added. A group of wild, frightened horses plunged out of a coulee and thundered down the road behind the stage. Coppers could make out two riders hazing the animals and waving white sheets.

The stage slowed, then plunged on as Humpy used his whip. The wild horses came on in confusion, snorting, whinnying, their eyes white with fright. Some of those horses in the rear had tin cans tied to their tails, adding to their terror.

The horse herd engulfed the stagecoach, spreading out into the open areas between house, barn, and corrals, crashing into fences, knocking over a small windmill that pumped water into the pasture. A half-dozen wild horses broke off from the main herd and plunged through the dude riders, exciting those horses, some of which began to buck and run. Humpy, standing up in the box of the stage, held in his own frightened hitch and lashed out at the wild horses with his whip.

Coppers was running out, toward the stage, waving his arms, feeling like a fool, trying to turn the wild horses. He angled away toward the horse pasture and found his way barred by a wild-eyed mustang. He grabbed it by the mane and swung up, sitting high on the withers, leaning over to get a grip on the foaming muzzle. He kicked his heels into the pony, twisted an upper lip, and the horse went bolting and bucking off through the herd, emerging on the far side, near the corral. A minute later Coppers was on his own horse, without a saddle, but in command of this one for it wore a hackamore. He drove the wild mustangs before him, as the two riders hazing the mustangs threw away their sheets, drew their guns, and began firing in the air. They managed to get off several rounds before Coppers responded and drove them out of sight into a shallow draw. Sheathing his gun, he continued to drive the bewildered and frightened mustangs up the draw, pushing them back into a shallow canyon.

In less than five minutes they were out of sight. In the distance he could hear the sounds of their passing, the rattle and clink of stones in the tin cans that had been tied to the tails of a few of them. He shook his head. Those horses would run themselves to death.

As he emerged from the shallow draw a cowhand rode up to Coppers and stuck out his hand. "Ain't seen nothin' like it since Cheyenne Frontier Days," he declared. "Some ridin', mister."

"Thanks," Coppers said dryly. "I'm some rusty. This how you salute all the returning guests?"

"Mister, Mel Bennion never had nothin' to do with that," the leathery-faced cowboy said earnestly. He shifted in his saddle.

"It'd be a sight to see you when you wan't rusty." He leaned his head toward the dudes, some of them standing and holding their horses, others sitting a nervous saddle. All of them bore the marks of days on the trail. "I'd just about give up hope for the hooman race till just this here minute. I gotta go now and do some dude tendin' but I'll see you around. You one o' Mel's new hands?"

"No. I work for the Slash B," Coppers said, wondering if he really did.

The man's face froze and he eyed Coppers narrowly. "That a fact?" he asked coldly. "Well, so long, friend." Raising his hand, he wheeled his horse and rode toward the group of waiting guest dudes.

CHAPTER THIRTEEN

Coppers rode around the dudes and stopped before the house where Mel Bennion stood, barefooted, directing the leathery-faced cowboy who'd earlier congratulated Coppers on getting the wild mustangs away from the guests.

"Get 'em to the guest houses," Bennion was saying. "Get 'em to hell anyplace, Grady. Get a fire ring goin' and we'll have a singfest right after supper. Music, lots of it and loud. An', dammit, Grady, either Spook or Rattle has got to go. Can't have 'em fightin' over lady dudes, hear me?"

"Yeah, boss, I hear. Rattle and Spook been buddies for four, five years. They'll get over their spat when the lady dude goes home. You want me to get rid of 'em? Both? Spook plays the gittar, remember."

"Oh, hell a mighty," Bennion groaned. "Bust 'em up for a spell, Grady. Get Rattle to ride fence till that flirty gal goes home." He wheeled and went limping toward the door, waving Sal aside, cursing as he stopped to lift a bare foot and remove a splinter.

Sal came down the steps, looking at Coppers, concern darkening her face and fear clouding her eyes. "Aletha—she's gone!"

Coppers stared at Sal, waiting for her to continue.

"She and Tommie . . . Tommie is so proud to be able to help her. The two of them . . . picking flowers, wild flowers, along the creek when all the racket started and those horses, those wild horses—"

"Does your husband know?"

She nodded. "He's got Tommie in the office. . . ." She turned away stumbling on the steps in her haste.

He was close behind her when she opened a door, motioning

him inside. Humpy, the hunchbacked cowboy slid through the door.

Bennion sat in a chair with Tommie between his knees. Tommie was crying, his face screwed up, his mouth open, as Mel Bennion held the boy's chin with his fingers so that Tommie had to look directly at him. Water from Tommie's clothing drained on the floor.

"Don't be scared, Tommie," Bennion said soothingly. "Nobody gonna hurt you. Just tell me what you—what happened."

Tommie rolled his eyes toward Coppers and even tried to smile.

"They took her," Tommie choked out. "Grabbed her, two men did. They had an extra horse. One of them rode by me and his stirrup hit me and knocked me in the creek."

"Which way did they go, Tommie?"

"Toward the mountains."

Bennion patted the little boy on the head, hugging him for a moment, before calling for Sal.

She came in, flustered.

"Get him in some dry clothes," Bennion said, and waited until Sal and Tommie left the room. He turned to Coppers. "I guess you're Dave?" He held out his hand. "Glad to meet y' but not like this."

Coppers shook hands with Mel Bennion, liking what he saw—a hearty, leathery man with a solid look of strength and character about him. "Guess I'd better telephone the deputy sheriff in Arapaho."

"Don't do that," Coppers said. "Al Hunter was killed the other night. Shot from out of the dark."

Bennion stared. "God a mighty damn! Maybe the sheriff will send somebody to take his place." He moved toward the door.

"No, it'll take too much time. I'm going after them. Right now."

"The hell you will! She was taken here on my place. I'll get some of the boys—"

"No! They'd ruin what tracks we might pick up. I'll agree to you going but nobody else."

"Boss, I got a look at them two," Humpy said. "One of them is a drifter name o' Spud Oliver."

That stirred Coppers' memory of his ride to Muddy Creek station, followed by two men, one of them called Spud. They were the two who'd roughed up Dakota before that.

"Don't know the name of the other one," Humpy continued, "but near's I can figger out from what I heard in town he is none other than Henry Eggert, an ol' buddy o' Butch Cassidy an' Henry dropped out of sight 'bout same time Butch did."

"Humpy, you go saddle two horses," Bennion said. "Me and Dave here is gonna go after 'em." He cursed roundly as he got his gunbelt and holster off the cluttered rolltop desk and strapped it on.

You're losing them all, Coppers told himself as he waited for the horses to come up while Bennion prowled the room, growling like an angry bear.

Coppers had no doubt of his own capacity for slogging through to an end, picking up revealing pieces of information, and putting it all together to complete the puzzle. Thus far, however, he had brushed elbows with three murders—Gage, Max Callum, and young Gil Tatum. And now this: a kidnaping in a country that revered women, even the ladies of the night. Was there a connection in all of this? he asked himself.

He had an instinctive feeling that there was something important that he was missing, that he should know, and didn't know. It was frustrating, maddening, especially the fact that he couldn't tuck it away out of his mind so as to concentrate all of his mind and physical strength on going after Aletha's abductors.

He heard Humpy's hail from outside and he led the way toward the horses.

Coppers and Bennion rode two of the best of the Box MB remuda. Not sprinters but rangy beasts with tremendous staying power. Mel, carrying the lantern, leaned from his saddle now and again to cut sign. They made slow time, going no more than a half dozen miles from the Box MB, since cutting west toward the mountains and picking up the trail.

Spud Oliver and Henry Eggert, if that's who they were, made no attempt to cover their tracks.

"They thinkin' of putting miles between them and us," Bennion guessed. "Come mornin' they'll start coverin' their tracks."

Coppers pressed on impatiently, saying nothing.

After a few attempts to draw information from Coppers, Bennion lapsed into a grouchy silence, only to break it with an angry outburst.

"Why in hell would them two crazy cowboys do any such thing?" he cried. "What in hell is the world comin' to?"

"I don't know about the world," Coppers said, "but I'm wondering about a raid like this one on your ranch."

Bennion sighed. "I thought something else until I found out Aletha had been taken. First off, I thought the cattle and sheep war had caught up with me. We got two old bulls around here, Will Talbot, the sheepman, and Scott Tyrell, the cattle king. Between them two, they're makin' people take sides. I thought the wild-horse raid was an attempt to get me to side in with Tyrell, but I reckon not. Whoever's got Aletha is doin' it for ransom. Old man Boynton's supposed to be pretty well off."

"I thought the cattle and sheep people had settled their differences."

"Yeah. Was so till them two old fools got to bumpin' heads. I got nothin' against sheep. Matter of fact I tried 'em for a while. Stupidest goddamn animal God ever made and I got so I couldn't stand the sight of 'em."

Coppers only half listened. He trusted Bennion but knew he couldn't confide in him. He was certain that these two men they trailed were the same two who had beaten Dakota. The old man had refused to tell Coppers why he'd been picked out for a brutal assault. Then these same two had followed him almost to Muddy Creek before abandoning the chase, apparently believing that Coppers was leaving that part of the range. They had suspected him of something but he had no idea what it was.

What a mixed-up mess, he told himself in disgust. It was maddening to realize there was information available but not to him. He suddenly realized how Aletha must feel in strange territory. He was just as blind as Aletha, in a sense.

The moon came out and gave them a small fraction of added light. Coppers moved ahead of Bennion, leading the way and checking the trail now and then.

"They're headin' straight for some of the roughest country around," Bennion said. "You'd think they'd stick to the trails to make better time."

Irritated, Coppers remained silent, slogging ahead. The moon set and it suddenly seemed darker than pitch. The lantern guttered and then went out.

"Out of oil," Bennion said in disgust, shaking the lantern close to his head. He hurled it off into the darkness where it landed on a rock, amid a tinny clatter and sounds of breaking glass.

The land rose steeply here, a layer of rock exposed, littered with small loose stones and debris from the surrounding sparse vegetation.

Coppers stopped his horse, dismounted, rolled a cigarette, and after lighting it used the match to briefly explore the surrounding darkness. Rock shelved back in, creating a windbreak. The wind, strong earlier, had subsided to an almost gentle sweep down the mountain. Coppers felt a moment of gratitude that Bennion had provided him with a worn mackinaw which was warm, though a bit tight through the shoulders.

"Not much to do but wait for daylight," Coppers said and began unloosening his saddle. He got the saddle on the ground, worked the blanket between his fingers so it wouldn't crust and stiffen and dropped it on top of the saddle, and then rubbed the horse down. There was very little graze around and the horse kept trying to wander off in search of food.

Coppers sat with his back against the rock, staring moodily out at the sky, trying to estimate the time of night from the star pattern.

Bennion settled beside him. "Good God, but it's cold," he complained. "We must be up pretty high to be so cold."

"Where do you suppose they're heading?"

"Beats hell out of me. There's an old line shack a few miles ahead, but sheepmen are probably using it. They move their woollies up there for summer feed 'bout this time of year. There's a hundred places them two bastards could hole up."

"They were traveling light. Maybe they prepared a place before they took Aletha."

"Could be," admitted Bennion. He was silent for a moment and then he said: "Why didn't you want me to telephone the law in Laramie? Or get the boys on the trail?"

"Takes too much time to organize a posse. And you'd be half the night yelling in that telephone trying to make somebody in

Laramie understand what happened on the Box MB. I thought we'd do better, just the two of us." He really would have preferred to go it alone but refrained from letting Bennion know of his true feeling. He felt irritable and edgy and wanting to go on, senseless though it was; time seemed to stand still. The stars hadn't moved very much since he took first note of their position in the sky. He could hardly bear sitting with Bennion on the side of the mountain, waiting for daylight. Yet, he told himself, the time could be used profitably—if he could get information from Bennion without arousing his suspicion.

"You got a nice place down there," Coppers said. "You do all the building yourself?"

"Me? Hell no. I can't saw a straight line and I can't drive a nail without bending it. I hired ol' Luke Teeters over Arapaho way to do all my building. Luke's a good carpenter and a stonemason, too. An' he had some good helpers."

"You must have been building about the time Boynton started at the old Rafter G," Coppers said. It was important to learn as much about Boynton as he could, without giving it away. His frustration deepened as he realized he knew so little about what originally had seemed to him as a relatively simple job.

"I'm noddin'," Bennion said from the darkness. "Yeah, 'bout same time."

"Did Luke build—or rebuild I should say—the Boynton place?"

"Nope, he sure didn't. Boynton hired Luke to do the whole thing. Then, when Luke was ready to go in and start tearin' down the old place, in order to build on the same spot, Boynton suddenly changed his mind."

"Who did build it? I call it the castle—Boynton's house, that is."

"Name fits all right. Boynton went back to Dakota—or maybe it was Minnesota—an' got a bunch of foreign fellers to come out and do the job for him. Them builders couldn't even talk American. An' talk about bein' put out, I thought old Luke would have a fit. So was I; because Luke waitin' around for Boynton to make up his mind kind of delayed my building plans."

"Those foreign builders—they still around?"

"No, they're not. They got the place finished and disappeared

same as when they got here. Sort o' like them irrigators who
come every year to irrigate the land. You never see them before
they get here, and you never see them leave. They just show up
one day, do their work, and are gone when it's finished. You
seem almighty curious about all this. Thinkin' about movin' into
this country?"

Coppers laughed. "Hardly. If ranches were selling for five dollars I couldn't buy a fence post."

Bennion liked to talk, but Coppers sensed that he'd had
enough of it. He kept silent as time dragged on. Bennion snored
and Coppers felt an unreasoning surge of anger toward him.
Coppers felt a twinge of guilt at his anger. Bennion had been on
the trail for a long, tiring ride with about thirty dudes. That was
enough to wear out a man even tougher than Bennion. He's a
good man, Coppers thought, who lived the way of Westerners.
Hospitable, a man of his word, quiet, efficient, and able to handle
most situations.

The sky lightened, darkened, and then the true dawn grayed
the sky toward the plains, and the stars winked out.

Coppers rose, stretching. His horse whinnied and pawed the
rocky ground. Bennion sat up, scrubbing his face with his two
hands, and put on his hat.

"Let's get on," Coppers said, and picking up his saddle blanket laid it on the back of the horse he was riding and smoothed
it out. He threw on the saddle and buckled the cinch. Bennion
silently saddled his own horse.

They came out of the shelter of the rocky bank, and Coppers
surveyed the shallow arroyo leading toward the summit of the
nearest mountain which was about a third of the line of foothills
before encountering the Rocky Mountains. The ground over
which they rode was almost solid rock. Coppers dropped his
reins and went forward on foot, searching every inch of the
ground, working his way back and forth across the bed of what
had once been an ancient stream. He found a few scratches in
the rock that could have been made by ironshod hoofs. A blade
of grass growing out of a crack in the rock had been crushed. He
squatted there on his heels, studying the ground, with a feeling
of impotent rage growing on him.

"Find anythin'?" Bennion asked.

Coppers stood up abruptly. "They went this way," he said and strode to his horse and mounted.

"I didn't bring anything to eat," Bennion said.

"There's jerky in my saddlebags," Coppers said snappishly. He was jumpy. Time was running out. The longer they delayed the farther along Spud Oliver and Henry Eggert would be taking Aletha.

He was heading out, but he checked his horse when a spatter of gunshots sounded distantly.

"Over the next ridge," Bennion said, his voice trailing off as Coppers put spurs to the big horse he rode.

Coppers kept the horse in a laboring run as he climbed the folds of the hills ahead, rising to the summit and looking down into the valley. The sun was with them briefly and as they began their descent they were again in a land of shadowy before-dawn limited light. The far mountains were bathed in sunlight from the morning sun. That's why they call them the shining mountains, he thought.

Coppers hauled up his mount with a scatter of gravel. A wagon was afire down there and burning fiercely; a sheepherder's wagon. Two bodies lay near the wagon and all around were gray humps—sheep that had been killed. The main flock was scattered far and wide across the valley. There was a cloud of dust lingering over one of the canyons branching off from the valley on the far side.

"Let's get on down," Coppers said as Bennion neared him. He dug in his spurs and the big horse broke into a hard, pounding run toward the burning wagon.

Two dogs were tied to the flaming wagon. Coppers cursed as he saw them struggling to escape the flames. He jumped to the ground, got out his knife, and slashed the ropes holding the two dogs; they crouched at his feet whining until he pointed and said, "Get 'em!"

The dogs scampered toward the sheep and began gathering them into a tight and huddled mass.

Bennion loped up and dismounted. He stared at the two men on the ground. "They're dead?"

Coppers walked over and squatted beside the nearest sheepherder. The man had been shot twice and had lived only long enough to stagger out of the wagon. The other herder was literally shot to pieces.

"Good God!" Bennion muttered. He walked over and picked up a round piece of heavy wood. "Looky, they busted spokes out of the wagon wheels and used 'em to club the sheep. Will Talbot's gonna have somebody's scalp for this piece o' work."

Coppers rose to his feet facing Bennion. "Talbot?"

"Yeah. Biggest sheepman these parts. You know him?"

Coppers shook his head, remembering how he and Harlan Gage had searched for Harlan's father, and, not finding him, had given him up for dead. Frank Gage had sought out Will Talbot for invading his range and never returned. Ancient history, he thought. "I don't believe those two who took Aletha did this," he said. "Just doesn't make sense." But then, he told himself, nothing at all made sense to him, not any longer.

"We'll have to let Talbot know," Bennion said.

"You let him know if you want to," Coppers said, and stepped into his saddle. "I'm keeping after those two—if I can pick up the trail."

"Well, hell, I'm not gonna let you go it alone," Bennion growled, mounting. "We'll get word to Talbot soon's we can; that's what I meant in the first place."

With Coppers leading they rode in silence back the way they'd come, looking for sign of the trail they'd abandoned to investigate the burning wagon. Coppers saw a glint of color beside a stunted pine. He rode to it and dismounted. He squatted in the shade of his horse, picking up a small, gray glove of some soft material. How tiny, he thought, fingering Aletha's glove. "She come by here," he said, when Bennion rode up behind him. "She left this glove."

"How'd she know?"

"Heard the sound of iron horseshoes on rock. Knew the horses wouldn't be leaving tracks. She probably dropped something else along the way. You ride ahead while I stand here, that way we'll go from sign to sign—if she did manage to drop something else." He put the glove in his shirt pocket and watched Bennion mount and ride slowly ahead, scanning the ground.

Taking the glove from his pocket, Coppers sniffed it, breathing deeply her familiar scent. That act brought an unfamiliar ache somewhere deep inside him, disturbing and unsettling.

Coppers straightened as he saw Bennion, in the distance, stand up in his stirrups and then lean from the saddle to retrieve something on the ground. He held it aloft, waving his arm.

Mounting, Coppers urged his horse up the slope.

"It's a little piece of blue ribbon," Bennion said, holding it out to Coppers.

Coppers took the soft bit, remembering she'd worn it in her hair, beneath the funny hat she'd so carefully pinned on before leaving the Slash B. Was it yesterday? It seemed a year ago. Coppers took the ribbon from Bennion and thrust it in his pocket with the glove. "It's hers," he said. "I'll ride ahead. You wait here."

Coppers urged his horse into motion, keeping a tight rein when the animal would have lunged up the steepening slope. He ranged back and forth, covering every inch of ground. He was ready to give up when he found the other glove. He looked back at Bennion, got a line of sight on the direction of travel, and then motioned the rancher toward him.

Coppers stared bleakly ahead, waiting for Bennion with impatience gnawing at him. When Bennion rode up, Coppers said, "I found another glove. That's the way they're heading." He motioned. "Any ideas?"

Bennion shifted in his saddle, the leather creaking. "There's an old abandoned mine up that near canyon, just over the top. Few shacks, maybe a dozen, and a hole in the side of the mountain that nobody ever took anything out of worth a plugged nickel. Eagle Springs, they called it when people were there. Now, it's a ghost town."

"There must be a road into the town," Coppers said.

"Comes in from the other side."

"How much farther?"

"Not more'n an hour, Dave. We ain't sure they're gonna hole up there."

"We'll find out," Coppers said shortly. "Go ahead."

He waited until Bennion rode past and then got his own horse into motion, thinking, If Aletha wasn't up there, I'd be leading instead of following. She was exerting a powerful influence on him and the realization shook him.

The more he saw of Bennion the more he liked the big rancher. Bennion was a strange mixture of exuberant kid and cautious wise rancher. Bet he was a heller when he was young, Coppers thought. Bennion lost no points with Coppers by marrying Sal. Women were few in the West; more than one had moved from the uncertain status of soiled dove to that of respectable wife and mother. That was the West at its very best, Coppers mused. A man, or a woman, was judged on what they were and not on what they claimed to have been at some past time in their lives.

Bennion stopped his horse and Coppers' mount halted of its own accord. Bennion swung in the saddle. "We're nearly there," he warned.

Coppers raised his head sniffing. "Smell smoke," he said.

Three canyons branched off from the shallow arroyo they'd climbed. There were tracks in the first clear imprintable area they had encountered.

The group they trailed had stopped here. Several piles of horse droppings attested to at least four horses. Two of the riders had dismounted and smoked. One of the riders had left the group, heading off over a saddle in the general direction of Arapaho.

Dismounting, Coppers stretched mightily. "What do you make of it?" he asked Bennion.

"Somebody sure as hell joined up with them. And then took off right about here. I don't know what to make of it." Bennion got down from his horse, groaning. "I'm hungrier'n hell."

Coppers ignored that. "What's the lay of the land?"

Bennion squatted. Picking up a dead stick he began tracing in the dirt. "Canyon twists and turns, closing in and getting steeper. Buckbrush, pine, and some quaking aspen. Good cover. We can circle and hit it from any side. I'll go with the shortest way."

"All right with me," Coppers said, rising and lifting his reins. "We walk from here on."

"You're a hard man, Dave," Bennion said.

A hawk swooped silently above them, looked them over and

sped away. Somewhere in the distance a quail sounded a warning of their approach; there was a roar of wings and a dozen
birds took to the air at the same time. A white-tailed deer leaped
out of cover just ahead of them, bounding away in great springy
leaps that carried it out of sight almost at once.

Coppers and Bennion stopped as one when the roof of a distant cabin showed above the ridge ahead. Coppers backed his
horse off the faint trail.

"Let's cut across here and try to keep out of sight," he said,
leading the way into rougher terrain, trying to avoid rocks so the
ironshod hoofs of the horses did not make a carrying sound.

Slowly they worked their way to a higher point so that almost
the entire ghost town lay spread out before them, tightly clustered almost at the very crest of the ridge that flattened on
top. Three horses stood before a large cabin but only one of
them was saddled.

Bennion sank to the ground, removing his hat and wiping his
forehead with his shirt sleeve. "That's the bunkhouse, where the
horses are," he said. "Cookshack right next to it. Rest o' them
cabins are family quarters."

"You seem to know."

"Yeah. When younger than now I had a girl friend who used
to cook for the mining company. I'd come up now and then in a
buggy and we'd go ridin'." Shaking his head, he added: "Long
time ago and it was a bustlin' lil town, now look at it."

A man came from the bunkhouse and mounted the saddled
horse. Another man emerged and stopped in the doorway, leaning the point of a shoulder against the frame, talking and gesturing. He took a few steps forward, looking up at the mounted
man, talking and making emphatic gestures.

"That's Henry Eggert, all right," Bennion said. "He's a bad 'un,
Dave."

"I wish I could hear what he's saying," Coppers said.

"Givin' orders, likely," Bennion offered.

Coppers agreed, nodding. He watched closely, tensing as the
mounted man pulled his animal around and rode away from the
bunkhouse. He soon passed out of sight in a wrinkle in the land
and reappeared a few minutes later.

"He's goin' back the way we come," Bennion said.

"Uh-huh. You stick here and watch, but I don't think they'll be leaving soon. I'll go on down to a place I remember and see about taking that fellow. We might get some answers." As he talked he unbuckled his spurs. He stood and removed the Colt from its holster and shoved it into the waistband of his pants. He unstrapped his gunbelt and dropped it on top of his spurs.

"Good huntin'," Bennion grunted and turned back to watch the bunkhouse as Coppers went down the mountain, walking swiftly but without making noise. He was in a different canyon than the rider who'd just left Eagle Springs, but he knew the two arroyos intersected down below.

Dave Coppers was thinking of one thing only. He wanted to get that rider alive and question him. After that was done, he could get back to Bennion and figure out how to get Aletha free of her abductors.

Coppers reached the place at the intersection of the two canyons and surveyed the possibilities. The faint trail curved around the upthrust of the ridge separating the two canyons. A rock shelf was naturally carved out of this ridge at just about head high of a man atop a horse. He climbed up and positioned himself, squatting on his heels, waiting. He could now hear the faint sounds of the approaching horse, growing louder.

The horse's head came into view and then the man, riding carelessly, his body swaying to the motion of the horse.

Suddenly the horse stopped, tossing its head and looking around, snuffling.

The rider came alert, rising in his stirrups, his head pivoting around from side to side, his hand resting on the butt of his gun. He was a hawk-nosed man of uncertain age, thin lips, near-white hair, and his alert, deepset eyes seemed like those of an animal peering from a dark cave.

Coppers tensed and then relaxed as the rider settled back into his saddle, kicking his horse in the ribs and cursing.

When he passed, Coppers leaned out and with a single blow of his Colt knocked the man from his saddle.

CHAPTER FOURTEEN

Coppers scrambled down from the rock ledge, while the horse trotted ahead for a dozen feet before stepping on its dragging reins which tugged him to a stop.

Coppers stooped over the man and removed the Colt from a well-worn holster. He rolled a cigarette and got it lighted and then smoking, squatted beside the unconscious man, and waited for him to come to his senses.

He saw an edge of brown paper sticking from the man's pocket and he slipped it out. The paper had been torn from a paper sack and the writing on it in heavy black pencil was easy to read:

PUT ALL OF THE MONEY (ALL OF IT) IN A SOOGAN. PUT OUT
A FLAG ON YOUR RANCH FLAGSTAFF WHEN YOU'RE READY TO DEAL.

Coppers shoved the ransom note in his shirt pocket and leaned down to look at the purpling lump above the man's ear. The gun frame had split the skin and a trickle of blood oozed from the slight wound. The man's thin blond hair was beginning to go and he had no forelock at all. After the examination, Coppers watched warily, showing no trace of the impatience gnawing at him.

Coppers was finishing his smoke when the man stirred. Coppers pinched out the fire, opened the brown paper, and let the tobacco blow away in the wind.

A feeble groan came from the unconscious man. He stirred, raising a hand toward his head. When his fingers encountered the egg-sized knot, he groaned again and jerked his hand away.

Rising, Coppers kicked him lightly in the ribs. The man sat up, moving slowly, opening and closing his eyes, finally squinting dazedly at Coppers.

"What's your name?" Coppers began.

"That's none o' your damn business."

Coppers kicked him again, not so lightly. "When I give a question I want an answer or I'll break every damn bone you got. What's your name?"

"I ain't—" Seeing the look in Coppers' eyes, the man changed his mind. "Gard. Buel Gard."

"That's more like it," Coppers nodded approvingly. "Who you work for, Gard?"

"Ain't workin' right now."

Coppers took the brown piece of sack from his pocket and unfolded it. "You was on your way to deliver this," he said. "So you're doing something for someone. That means you're working for somebody. That means you're working, Gard, and I'm asking one more time—who's paying you?"

Gard hesitated, his hand protectively cupping the lump on his head. "Henry Eggert give me ten dollars to carry this to the Slash B. That's all I know."

Coppers pointed to the blood splashes on the man's lower legs and boots. "Where'd that come from?"

"Where'd what come from?"

"The blood on your clothes and boots."

"I helped a man butcher—"

Coppers pulled his gun and leaning over tapped the man lightly on his head. "You've done no honest work in your day," he said. "Did you kill those sheepherders—and the sheep?"

"I didn't kill nothin'," Gard denied in a sullen tone.

Coppers hit him again with the gun barrel. Gard ducked away but was not quick enough. "Hey, owtch, that hurt! Knock it off, dammit."

"You sonofabitch I'm going to beat you to death, little by little," Coppers said, all the more terrible because of his calm. "I want answers and I want 'em now. I'm in a hurry." He raised the Colt and Gard tried to move away but Coppers stepped on his ankle, bringing him to a stop and eliciting a yelp of pain.

"Wait now, and get off my foot. Me and my partner, Otis Finlay, we made a deal with Henry Eggert to carry this here note to old man Boynton, but we made another deal before that with Scott Tyrell to mess up the sheepherders. We went into the sheep camp and rounded up the herders—"

"You killed those two herders and you tied their dogs to the wagon intending to burn them alive. And then you killed the sheep."

Gard didn't look at Coppers and said nothing.

"Who does Henry Eggert work for?" Coppers asked.

Answering eagerly, Buel Gard said, "I don't know, I swear to God I don't know."

"You'd better tell me all of it—everything. Start talking."

Leaning over, Gard tried to puke but nothing came up.

Coppers watched pitilessly.

Gard wiped his nose on his dirty shirt sleeve and looked furtively at Coppers. What he saw was not reassuring.

"Me and my partner, Otis, we heard that Scott Tyrell was looking for a couple good men—"

"Killers you mean. Where were you when you heard all this?"

"Over Brown's Hole way. We come on up to Arapaho and was waitin' 'round for Mr. Tyrell. He finally come to town and we talked to him. He hired us to scare the sheepherders and maybe kill a few sheep. Just before we left town, Henry Eggert bought us a drink in the Wild Belle—that's a saloon—"

"I know what it is."

"Well, he bought us a drink, said he had a little job for us. We told him we had a job awready. He said his job wouldn't take long an' for us to meet him at Eagle Springs. Thass all there is to it, I swear."

"What was you supposed to do after delivering the note?"

Gard hesitated and when Coppers raised the pistol he spoke quickly. "I was to lay out in the brush and watch the Boynton house. When the flag went up, I was s'posed to go to a place up the river from Horsehead Crossing. Thass where Henry Eggert said he'd be camped."

"You know what's in that note you were carrying?"

Gard shook his head. "I—I can't read," he mumbled. "I never went to school, mister, an' that's God's truth."

"Where's your partner?"

"Me an' him split up," Gard said. "I guess he put in with Henry Eggert. I don't know what they're up to."

Coppers rose and walked to Gard's horse. He pulled the rifle from the saddle boot. "Get on your horse and get out of here," he said. "I see you again I'm going to kill you, Gard."

Gard climbed to his feet and shambled to his horse. He didn't look at Coppers until he was mounted. He cast a quick glance at Coppers, but the set of the big man's face caused him to forget what he was going to say. He slapped his reins against his horse's neck and rode away without looking back.

Shouldering Gard's rifle, Coppers started back up the mountain, going the same way he'd come down. He crouched down as he neared Bennion, to keep from being skylined. He crawled the last few feet.

For an instant the two men stared at each other and the expectant look on Bennion's face deepened. "You do all right?"

Nodding, Coppers crawled past Bennion, looking down into the old mining camp. He felt a sudden prickling on his scalp. Aletha sat outside the cabin with a guard nearby. He could hear the pound of his heart. He started up, but Bennion put out a restraining hand.

"Don't go off half-cocked," he said.

Coppers sank back into the ground, staring. "Seeing her kind of made me crazy," he said.

"Yeah, yeah," Bennion said irritably. "What'd you find out down there?"

Coppers took the ransom note from his pocket and passed it to Bennion, still looking at Aletha. His fear for Aletha was replaced with a cold rage that made it difficult to sit there on the mountain waiting for Eggert to make a move.

"Dave, I never heard tell of a woman bein' kidnaped in this country," Bennion complained. "Ol' Boynton don't have all that much money. . . . At least I think he doesn't." He returned the note to Coppers.

Coppers didn't enlighten Bennion. It was possible, he told himself, that Boynton had custody of close to two million dollars in real money. Real, that is, except for the missing signature of the U. S. Treasurer. It was a fact that some of the money had appeared in various cities in the West. There was a strong possibility that Professor Lemuel Taylor was the contact in Denver for distributing the partially forged paper money. Coppers had a flickering thought that he'd have been better off in every way if he'd heeded Ida Mae Courtney's wishes and settled in Washington, D.C. It was not a serious thought.

"Whether Boynton has money or not doesn't matter, not now, no," Coppers said in a deadly voice that caused Bennion to look up quickly as Coppers continued: "They've got Aletha. That's what matters now." *What in hell am I saying?* he thought.

"Steady now, Dave," Bennion warned. "Don't go doin' anything hasty like."

Henry Eggert emerged from the cabin carrying blanket rolls and saddlebags which he dumped on the ground. Spud Oliver rose lazily and began saddling the horses. Aletha continued to sit on a stump, her shoulders back and head erect.

"What the hell they up to?" Bennion asked snappishly.

"Buel Gard, he's the one I talked to down below, Mel. He told me he was supposed to hide out at the Slash B after he'd delivered the note. And when the flag went up, he was to ride to Horsehead Crossing, turn upstream for a piece, where Eggert will be camped. They'll give Boynton his orders then."

Bennion laid his Winchester across a rock and sighted in on Spud Oliver. "I believe I could kill both of them before they could get out of the way," he said, looking stolidly at Coppers.

"Aletha might get hit by a glancing bullet. They might even kill her. Can't risk it. Anyway, Mel, I want Henry Eggert alive. There's just one thing bothers me."

"What's that?"

"There should be one more man around. Otis Finlay. Gard told me that he and Otis came up this way together to work for Tyrell or Talbot, whichever paid the highest. That's what he said and I almost believe him. So where is Otis now?"

Bennion shrugged. "Can't guess. All I know is that he's the most cold-blooded sonofabitch alive. Not twenty-five years old and he's got a man for every year he's lived. That's not countin' Mexicans and Indians, Dave. Finlay thinks no more of killin' a man than he does shootin' a jackrabbit."

Coppers rolled a cigarette and after lighting it stuck the match into the dirt. He smoked moodily, thinking of the string of events since getting off the train in Cheyenne. That day such a short time ago seemed much longer. Harlan Gage shot down; finding

Max Callum dead in the ashes of his cabin on Warbonnet Road. The death of Gil Tatum, the younger stranger on the trail north, and why was he killed? Coppers' meeting with Aletha and the incident of the mountain lion, all these and more crowded into his mind, building his impatience and rapidly growing sense of frustration. And don't forget Al Hunter.

One of the men—it was Henry Eggert—stood looking up at the ridge behind which Coppers and Bennion sprawled. Coppers had a feeling that the man had been drawn to something there. He waited, watching with his eyes not directly on Eggert. He shoved his rifle into place.

Henry Eggert stepped away from his horse and was looking across the canyon to the ridge concealing Coppers and Bennion. Coppers knew he could not be seen from that distance, among the broken rock, the buckbrush, and spindly pines.

Eggert walked a few more feet and stopped. Lucky for you, Coppers thought. Another dozen feet and I'd have nailed you dead center.

"They're leavin'," Bennion announced.

Eggert was talking to Aletha. He touched her arm and she rose to her feet and walked to the horse where Eggert helped her to mount.

"What's to do?" Bennion asked.

"Down the canyon, there's a rockslide," Coppers said, remembering the place. "Loose rock in there. They'll be paying attention to getting across the slide. We might be able to surprise them." He buckled on his gunbelt and spurs.

"Whatever you say," Bennion said doubtfully.

They headed out down the canyon, which was separated by a rocky ridge from the canyon Eggert, Oliver, and Aletha would be traversing. They walked, leading their horses. There was time to spare as Eggert and his party had a longer distance to travel.

Moving without haste, they made their way down the canyon, through clumps of quaking aspen and pine, across small grassy meadows, and over barren rock. Coppers stopped now and then to listen and to survey the area.

Moving ahead toward the intersection of the two canyons, Coppers could see the tail end of the rockslide, just ahead, not more than a quarter of a mile. He came to the slide, skirted the edge of it, and they took cover under an old, old cedar tree whose branches spread almost to the ground.

Coppers kneeled there, looking out, waiting for the sound of the approaching horses. A turn in the canyon would screen them until Eggert was not more than a hundred feet away and in easy rifle shot. He checked his Winchester and saw Bennion do likewise.

Even though Coppers was expecting them, the lead rider emerged suddenly into view, the horses slowing as they picked their way carefully through the talus. When they were near as they'd come, Coppers yelled: "Stop right there. We got you covered!"

All the horses stopped as one. For a moment the entire scene was frozen, motionless. Then Spud Oliver simply rolled out of his saddle and as he was falling his rifle came up.

Coppers caught his front sight on the yellow drawstrings of a Bull Durham sack in the man's breast pocket and squeezed off a shot, feeling the rifle buck in his hands. Oliver raised up for a moment, slumped back, and lay still.

Without losing more than a second, Coppers turned his rifle on Eggert but Bennion got off his first shot knocking the man's hat off.

Henry Eggert was blindly firing his pistol in their general direction, and Coppers heard the sound of bullets bouncing off the rocks. "Try not to kill him," he said to Bennion and aimed for Eggert's horse. The animal Eggert rode was going wild under the spur and the sharp rocks biting into the sensitive flesh between the horseshoes.

Suddenly Eggert was gone, out of sight, down the canyon, his horse clear of the rockslide and running hard.

"Wait," Coppers called as Bennion ran toward his horse. "I know where to find him." He moved out from the cedar tree and began running toward Aletha, sitting her horse, waiting.

She heard the pound of his boots and flinched.

"It's all right," he called. "It's all over, Aletha."

He came to her and took her hand, warm and soft, lying in his own big fist without a tremor. Her face was calm though pale. "I knew you'd come," she said simply.

He resisted the urge to take her out of the saddle and hold her close to him, a wild impulse that came from nowhere. Instead, he gathered her reins and said, "We're in a rockslide here. We'd better get on sounder ground."

"Yes, Dave," she said.

Bennion came up. "Oliver's dead," he said.

"Eggert was the one I wanted," Coppers said, leading the horse out of the rocks. He stopped just below the cedar tree where they'd taken shelter and helped Aletha to the ground. She brushed against him and he steadied her. "Are you all right, Aletha?" he asked with concern. "Did they mistreat you?"

"It wasn't very pleasant, Dave, but after sobering up they treated me well. It was just a drunken prank, I'm sure."

He stared at her incredulously and then decided not to disagree with her, though he did think otherwise. "I'll be busy a few minutes," he told her. "I'll be near, though, and you're safe here." He took off his mackinaw and spread it on the ground and helped her to a seat.

Smiling, she said, "I felt safe the moment I heard your voice."

Coppers nodded to Bennion and they walked together to Spud Oliver's body. The man was sprawled on the rocks, cradling his rifle in his arms.

"I don't want to do this," Coppers said; "it's a job for the law. But I've got to find out all I can."

Kneeling, Coppers went through Oliver's pockets and found no more than the usual assortment of trivia a cowboy carried: a few horseshoe nails, a pocketknife, a plug of Pic Nic Twist chewing tobacco, and a half pint of whiskey.

"Just who the hell are you?" Bennion abruptly asked.

Coppers didn't answer at once but leaned over and pulled Oliver's shirt out of his pants. He found a money belt. It contained two hundred dollars in gold and greenbacks.

"You gonna answer me?"

"I'm a cowhand, nothing more," Coppers said mildly.

"Bull hockey! I might spend a lot o' time ridin' herd on a bunch o' dudes, but I hear things even out on the Box MB."

"So?"

Bennion made a sound of strong doubt. "Listen, Dave, you're

closemouthed an' maybe you listen good. There's word goin' around that since you got to these parts some men have been killed under mysterious circumstances. You workin' for Talbot or Tyrell?"

"I'm not in any sheep and cattle trouble," Coppers said shortly. "If I was, I'd tell you, Mel."

Bennion looked at him long and hard. "Well, I guess that's good enough for me," he said reluctantly. "Sal thinks an awful lot o' you and that means somethin' to me, too."

Coppers began piling rocks on Oliver's body. "This'll keep for a few days, what with these cold nights. Let somebody know, Mel." He stood up and looked at Bennion. "We can't tell anyone but the law."

Bennion shook his head. "You can't keep something like this quiet."

"In time," Coppers said briefly. "You'll take care of it?"

"I'll send one of the boys to Arapaho soon as I get home. Sal's worryin' 'bout Aletha, I know, and I want to tell her Aletha is fine."

Bennion turned away but Coppers detained him, a troubled look on his face. "What you said about men dying since I showed up—there's more than you know about and I'm worried. Not for me but for anybody seen with me. I'm caught in the middle of this, Mel, and don't know what to do."

"However I can help, you can bank on it."

"I don't know if you can. See, if someone is tracking me—and if there is, he's the best damn skulker in the business—it means that anybody I talk to or spend any time with is in danger. That's you, Mel. And Aletha."

Bennion wrinkled his forehead and shook his head. "It's all too much for me, I do declare," he said.

"Just be damn careful riding home," Coppers said. "Don't relax for a minute. After I get Aletha back to the Slash B, I'm riding on to Horsehead Crossing. I'll wait for Eggert to show up there."

"You think he will?"

"He doesn't know I got to Buel Gard. He'll probably try to collect the money."

"Where in the hell is Lute Farnell and his crew?" Bennion raged. "Why wouldn't he be out lookin'—"

"Maybe he doesn't even know Aletha was taken," Coppers said, not believing it at all. He was sure that somehow the slick cowboy was involved in this shenanigan.

CHAPTER FIFTEEN

Coppers and Aletha rode side by side, the horses walking, the sun warm on their faces. Aletha wanted to talk but Coppers was not so inclined.

He was more alert than he'd ever been in his life. Too many people had died within the time period of his unloading from the train in Cheyenne and this day. Mysterious, unexplainable killings from ambush.

Coppers rode with all his senses sharpened, paying special attention to areas where a man might lie in wait for a victim. At times he had Aletha wait while he rode ahead to examine a potential hideout for a killer.

When he returned from his latest scout, she said, "Wait," and urged her horse closer to him. "You're worried about what?"

He dismounted and adjusted his cinch that didn't need adjusting. "I'm tightening my cinch," he said. He'd learned to explain what she obviously could hear but perhaps not understand.

"You didn't answer me."

"Yes. Yes, I'm worried. For your safety." He dallied a while longer with the cinch, loath to ride on.

"There was shooting back there," Aletha said.

"Always that from time to time," Coppers answered. "Did you hear shooting just after daylight this morning."

She hesitated, then nodded.

"Want to tell me about it?"

"We'd been riding for some time. I really don't know how long. But I can tell the difference between daylight and dark. And it was light when the shooting began. Shortly after that, someone joined us. I had to give up my horse and ride double with Mr. Eggert."

"Who was it joined up with you?"

"I don't know. When they talked they went away, so distant I couldn't hear what was being said. Then we went on and the man who joined us went away in another direction." She moved impatiently. "Now, what about the shooting while I was riding through the shale?"

"Kidnaping is bad enough anywhere, but out here in this country—" He broke off, his unspoken words more eloquent for the trailing silence.

"It was just a prank," she said. "They were under the influence of strong drink. When they sobered up, they realized the seriousness of it and we were on our way home."

"Did they tell you that?"

She shook her head. "No, I assumed it. These fun-loving cowboys are rather like children."

"They're dangerous children," Copper said sternly. "They are killers, some of them. I'm certain they were not playing games."

"Did someone get hurt?"

Coppers didn't answer.

"Your silence means someone was hurt. A man killed, perhaps?" She shivered.

"When men commit serious crimes in this country, it's not like back East in the big cities. There, you call a policeman and he takes care of everything. Out here every honest man must be his own policeman. Sometimes it's kill or be killed."

"Do you think the West will change, become tame?"

"It is changing. But there are certain values here that I hope will go on forever."

"Such as?"

Coppers shrugged, embarrassed by his thoughts. "Self-reliance for one thing. Neighborliness—Mel Bennion didn't have to come with me; he wasn't forced to do it. He'd have brought his whole crew if I'd of let him. Freedom to move around. The worth of a man, woman, or child for what he or she is and not what they pretend to be."

"You sound like our President Roosevelt."

"He was attracted to the West," Coppers admitted. "He subscribes to self-sufficient people."

"You make all this sound like it is such a secure world."

"I don't mean to. The security is there for those who make it secure. A man has to be willing."

"Willing to do what?"

"To kill if necessary," Coppers said grimly, "to keep what's rightfully his own or to protect those he loves—or someone he is responsible for."

She shook her head from side to side. She had a smudge of dirt on one brown cheek and her hat was awry but she still appeared beautiful to Coppers. She said, "I don't know if I can accept that."

"Maybe in time," he murmured and leather squeaked as he mounted his horse. She urged her horse near him. She put out her hand, groped for a moment. Her small brown hand covered his hand resting on the saddle horn.

"Please don't worry for my sake," she said.

He sucked in his breath, looking long and openly at her in all her fresh beauty and womanly curves, feeling an ache somewhere that went way beyond his growing concern for her safety. He wished suddenly that he was free of the Secret Service, that he was obligated to no one in the world other than this lovely woman who rode by his side. "I can't promise you anything," he said.

He continued to be cautious as they moved on. He watched the land around dotted with pine and buckbrush, the rocky arroyo and side canyons. He wasn't worried about himself; his concern was directed toward the safety of this slim beautiful woman who affected him more strongly than anyone had previously affected him in all of his life. They walked their horses into the ranch house, just before sundown, stopping before the castle.

He helped her from the horse and she said, "Please come in for a little while." He tethered the horses and moved close to her and she took his arm. They walked up the steps, crossed the porch, and went inside. Coppers closed the door. She dropped her hand from his arm but didn't move away, turning so as to more fully face him. "You're not the same man who rescued me from the cat, Dave."

"I feel no different."

"But you are. We sightless people—we compensate for our blindness by using our other senses more fully. You were so kind and gentle on the trail, the day I met you. Now you're hard, ruthless."

"Conditions are different. Everything is different. There's a mystery here that bothers me. I don't like mysteries."

"Life is full of them. Which one worries you most of all?"

"You being kidnaped. Puzzle number one: Lute Farnell. I suspect he had something to do with it."

"Dave, that's not true! I can't believe it."

She's protecting him, Coppers thought, just as she stood up to Farnell for me. He recognized a boiling up of jealousy.

"I can't prove it," Coppers admitted. "But just to be on the safe side, I'll watch him."

"You're not a man who works the safe side," she said.

He moved restlessly and from the expression on her face he knew she heard his movements. "I've got to take care of the horses," he said. "Tomorrow I'll return Bennion's horse and bring Farah back." After that was done with, he meant to ride to Horsehead Crossing for a confrontation with Eggert.

"Each time you leave I wonder if you'll be back," she said.

"Don't worry about that; I'll be back. I should talk to your grandfather."

"You're not going to tell him about this?"

"He should know; he has a right to know."

"You must not tell him!"

He studied her determined face uncertainly.

Aletha stood on tiptoe and kissed his cheek, her hand resting on his shoulder. "Thank you, Dave," she breathed. She moved away from him, walking toward the stairway, grasped the bannister and began ascending. She paused at the top of the stairs and turned for a moment in his direction before disappearing.

It was full dark when Coppers went outside and untied the horses to lead them to the barn. The wind was stronger now, blowing steadily out of the southwest, with occasional gusts. As he walked the horses to the barn he saw lights in the upstairs windows. Aletha recovering from a harrowing experience; just how bad had it been? She didn't appear flustered and, except for the smudge of dirt on her cheek and slightly rumpled appearance, seemed none the worse.

He stopped so suddenly the horses bumped him and his Colt appeared in his hand.

"It's me," Dakota said quickly, coming forward. "You sure got that gun out in a hurry, man."

Coppers sheathed his weapon. "Don't come up on me like that," he said.

"I been watchin' for you," Dakota said. He held out something to Coppers. "These here telegrams come in the mail. Was sent to Laramie and the Laramie operator mailed them to Arapaho. Ol' man Dexter give 'em to me to give to you."

Coppers jammed the mail in his pocket and went forward, looping the reins over his arm as he got a lantern from a nail beside the door and lighted it. He held the lantern up and looked at Dakota as the old man sidled near.

"I ain't never been one to give out advice, but you'd better move on, mister."

"What, you too?"

"Huh? You're in for a lotta grief you stick here, bucko. I can't tell you any more'n that, but you can bet on it. I like you, Dave. You gone outta your way to he'p me and I ain't one to forget things like that. Take a tip from an ol' man who ain't so smart and make tracks."

Coppers only wanted to be rid of Dakota so he could read his mail. He said, "I'll think on it, Dakota. Thanks for tipping me off."

"But you ain't about to do nothin' about it," Dakota declared. "You young fellers always know it all till you're in a bind and then it's usually too late. Well, don't say I didn't tell you. . . ." He was still mumbling as he walked away toward the dark bunkhouse.

Where's Slim and Farnell, Coppers wondered as he placed the lantern on the ground and squatted there, opening one of the letters, looking at the sweeping scrawl of the telegraph operator who had transcribed the original message:

As of this date you are relieved of all responsibility for the case assigned you. Report at once to Antlers Hotel, Cheyenne, to await further orders. Raven.

Coppers pushed his hat to the back of his head. This, he thought, doesn't add right. Agency procedure dictated that all communications, orders, directives, and memos originating in headquarters would be signed by Effington, or Effington's code name. Raven was Buford Skiles's code name.

What, he wondered, had happened in headquarters? Had Skiles replaced Effington? He didn't know and there was no way he could find out in a hurry.

He opened the second envelope and found it to be in the clear also (uncoded) originating in the Denver office of the Secret Service.

Lemuel P. Taylor, not an alias, b. Virginia of respectable well-to-do parents, now deceased, was briefly employed by Treasury Department following expulsion from William and Mary during junior year. Background reveals Taylor arrested and convicted of misappropriation of printed money scheduled to be destroyed, sentenced to five years hard labor. Through intercession of Treasury official, Alexander Boynton, lifetime friend of Taylor family, LPT paroled and then headed west, where he has been active in variety of con games over the years. Currently involved in small time operation, teaching music to church groups, minor theatricals, and is booking agent for road shows appearing in Denver. Has been known to consort with violence oriented element, particularly dangerous and reputedly crazy killer named Finlay, Otis, AKA Amarillo Pete. Taylor presently absent from Denver, said to be at or enroute Arapaho, Wyoming. Agent No. 37.

At about the same time Coppers and Bennion were prowling the ruined sheep camp, Buford Skiles, second man in the Secret Service, Washington, D.C., rapped on Chief Effington's office door and entered, carrying the usual handful of papers.

Effington scarcely seemed to notice him, staring vacantly out of the window.

Skiles waited patiently, watching Effington lean back and search his breast pocket for a cigar. He inserted the cigar in his mouth and then discovered a still-smouldering, half-smoked cigar in his artillery-shell ashtray. With a vexed exclamation, he dropped the cigar on his desk and took up the other from the ashtray to puff it furiously.

Effington swung his chair around and without looking at Skiles, said, "Yes, Buford, what is it?"

"I'm afraid Coppers is in trouble, Chief," Skiles said.

"Coppers? Trouble. Come, man, tell me what you're talking about."

"You recall we dispatched Coppers to Wyoming—"

"Of course, of course," Effington said, waving his cigar. Effington had got an upsetting telephone call that morning from President Roosevelt's secretary. The President, the secretary informed him icily, wanted Effington in his office at 1 P.M. and Effington had not the slightest idea what was in store for him. He'd never had a White House call before; and, he thought, I hope I never get another. He was more than uneasy at the impending visit to the President. The man, beloved by most Americans, was an unpredictable sort. One never knew what he was up to at any given moment.

Effington realized with a start that Skiles had been talking rapidly for some time and he forced himself to concentrate on what his second in command was telling him. "I think it would serve the agency well if I travel to Wyoming," Skiles was saying. "I believe that decisive action is called for at once. This needs resolution at the highest level possible."

Good God, Effington thought, what is the man babbling about? "You haven't had field experience, Skiles," Effington said. He used his assistant's last name when he was displeased with him.

"That's the purpose," Skiles said stubbornly. "I mean to make the most of this field trip. You know we've discussed it in the past, many times."

"Ah, yes, do what you think best," Effington said, suddenly tired beyond belief. That's ridiculous, he thought, I haven't done a damn thing today to make me so tired.

"Wait a moment, Buford," Effington said as Skiles turned away from his desk. "You're familiar with President Roosevelt, certainly as familiar as most. Is he a genius or a half-wit?"

"Some of both," Skiles said promptly. "He has all the attributes of one and of the other, I'm afraid."

Effington almost groaned. "Is he crazy?"

"Like a fox, sir."

"Do you believe all the stories you hear of him? God knows they're endless."

"There's truth in most of them. What have you heard?"

"You're aware he's very, very partial to his former Rough Riders, those who went with him to Cuba?" Without waiting for Skiles's assent he continued: "Roosevelt gave them permission, encouraged them, really, to call on him at the White House, any time of day or night. One of his Western roughnecks did just that and was turned away. When Roosevelt learned of it he was furious. When this fellow finally got to see the President, Roosevelt told him that if such a thing ever happened again, the cowboy was to fire his pistol through a White House window."

"I believe it, Chief," Skiles said. "For instance, one of his Rough Riders was sentenced to the penitentiary for murder. Roosevelt pardoned him—and made him warden of the prison he was released from."

Effington nodded, dismissing Skiles with a worried frown.

Alone once more, Effington drummed his fingers on his desk, trying to visualize his coming meeting with Roosevelt. Whatever in the world would the President of the United States of America want with the chief of Secret Service?

He pondered the question, thinking for a short time of the advisability of calling on the Secretary of the Treasury, his own boss, and asking for guidance. He abandoned the idea at once. He'd hardly spoken to the man since his appointment by Roosevelt to the Treasury post.

I've got to broaden my acquaintance, he thought in desperation, but it helped not at all at this particular moment.

CHAPTER SIXTEEN

When Coppers stepped inside the bunkhouse, he saw Lute Farnell, apparently bored, sitting at the table cleaning his pistol.

He laid the pistol aside watching Coppers, never taking his eyes from him. Slim lay on his bunk, staring at the ceiling, his head cradled in his clasped hands. Dakota was cross-legged on his bunk dealing out cards in his endless game of solitaire.

Farnell picked up the pistol, held the muzzle close to his eye, peering down the barrel. "What made you come back?" he asked curiously.

Coppers never took his eyes from Farnell as he thought of the strong possibility that Farnell more than likely had a hand in Aletha's kidnaping. He thought of Aletha thrown on a horse and forced to ride off into the night, not knowing what was in store for her. The thoughts seething in his brain caused his black eyes to glitter while a fury burned inside him. This thinking put a cruel shape on Coppers' mouth. Farnell saw it there and stiffened in his chair, an alertness possessing him.

"I asked you a question," Farnell said.

"I had no intention of leaving," Coppers said, the need for action becoming stronger and stronger, giving rise to his posture and the setness of his hard-featured gaze.

Farnell relaxed slightly. "Just as well," he said easily.

"Just as well for you or me?"

Farnell's alertness returned. He was puzzled, but he knew when he was being challenged and a gleam of joy came to his eyes as he began rising.

Coppers tipped the table over, pinning Farnell for a moment to the wall. He swept Farnell's gun to the floor and drove his fist into Farnell's face. The blow made a hard ugly sound. Farnell rebounded from the wall, falling to the floor.

Coppers stood there looking down at him, his lips drawn over his teeth. "Come on, tough guy," he said. "Get up and get the rest of it."

Slim was sitting on the edge of the bed, his hands on his knees. Dakota stopped his game, staring in fascination. Farnell slowly got to his hands and knees, shook his head and looked up dazedly. Blood trickled from his nostrils and his mouth. He turned his head, spat, and then came up, lunging and swinging. His blind rush carried Coppers across the room and against the opposite wall, shaking the bunkhouse to its foundations, causing the oil lamp to flicker. Coppers twisted aside and drove a hard fist into Farnell's face, deliberately trying to mar his too handsome features. Farnell expelled blood and spit gustily and fell back, trying to cover his face. Coppers followed, beating him about the head with hard, wild-swinging fists, oblivious to everything except to batter Farnell into the floor. Farnell, trying to recover, bulled into him, trying to pin his arms, while trying to stamp Coppers' feet.

Coppers threw his full weight against Farnell and they crashed to the floor locked together. Bunk braces gave way as they rolled over and over and the bunk crashed down. Farnell wiggled away, scrambled to his feet, coming up with a piece of heavy wood from the bunk. He brought it down with a vicious swing. Coppers rolled out of the path of the stick of wood and kicked out, connecting with Farnell's knee and at the same time throwing a powerful punch which landed on Farnell's jaw and knocked him flat.

Coppers, breathing hard, stood swaying, a wild light in his eyes, his black hair hanging over his eyes. He shook his head and looked around. He pointed at Slim.

"You want some of the same?"

Slim's face unfroze into a twisted grin and his pale eyes lighted up. "Reckon maybe I would," he said, "but I do my fighting with this." His hand streaked down as he tried to draw from a sitting position.

Dakota yelled, "Slim, don't do it!" The sound of Dakota's pistol going to full cock had a freezing effect on Slim.

In a softer voice, Dakota said, "Jus' take it easy, boy, if you want to live a lil longer."

"You puttin' in with him?"

"Ain't puttin' in with nobody right now," Dakota said. "I jes' ain't aimin' to have you shoot down a man without a gun. He lost his'n when he hit Lute that powerful wallop."

Slim struggled, slowly regaining control of his rage. He took his hand away from the butt of his pistol. Looking hard at Coppers, he said, "He'll be heeled sometime," and wheeled away, striding toward the door.

"Wait there," Coppers commanded.

Slim stopped but remained facing the door.

"Take Farnell out to the water trough and bring him around."

Slim stood there silently, his back stiff for a long-reaching moment, and then turned and went to Farnell. He took Farnell under his arms and dragged him out through the open doorway.

Coppers walked to the door and slammed it shut. He went through the bunkhouse to the back porch. He poured water from the bucket into a tin washbasin and washed blood from his face and chest, noting sourly that it wasn't all Farnell's blood. He dried himself and went back inside the bunkhouse.

Dakota sat on the bunk twirling his Colt by its trigger guard in studied concentration.

"Thanks for taking a hand," Coppers said gruffly.

Dakota executed a road agent's toss and holstered his weapon. "Jes' returnin' a favor," he said, sighing. He looked at Coppers. "You're purty much a damn fool, y' know it? I tole you to ride on, bucko, and it still goes."

"I've got a job here," he said. "Miss Aletha and Mr. Boynton both said so. And I kind of like the idea." He began shucking off his clothing. When he was down to his long johns, he stepped out of his boots and crawled into his bunk.

Dakota chuckled. "As they usta say in the olden days, you step on a rattler you liable to git bit."

Coppers answered with a snore.

Dakota chuckled again and said aloud, "I'll be dad-burned."

Dakota felt his years as he rode toward Arapaho with another package of memoirs for Professor Taylor. He could remember clearly how it had been down in Panguitch when he was in his early teens. Everything had been different then, the skies bluer, the clouds puffier and whiter, the grass greener, the birds even sang sweeter.

Now all the world was gray and dark and he could remember nothing of what happened yesterday or last week. But forty years ago—well, that was clear as a bell to him.

His horse stopped and Dakota came out of his reverie and saw Farnell and Slim at the ford, standing their horses beside the creek where they'd watered them. Water dripped from the horses' muzzles and Farnell's mount inched toward a blade of grass only to have its head pulled up sharply.

"You daydreamin' again, old man?" Farnell said.

"Yeah, I reckon." Dakota looked from one to the other, puzzled by their attitude. He also noted that Farnell's face was marked with purple bruises, a black eye and split lip, all the damage caused by Coppers' fists.

"We ready to make a move," Farnell said. "I guess it'll come off late today or early tomorrow."

"I've changed my mind," Dakota said. "I'm pullin' out, Lute. I want no part of it. He's not your man."

"I got proof," Farnell said, smiling. "I got too much ridin' on this deal, Dakota, to have you quit now."

"Maybe you have got proof," Dakota said slowly, "but like I told you, I ain't goin' along. Coppers is a good, decent man and I'll not have anythin' to do with it, not no more I won't."

Slim urged his horse across the creek and rode beyond Dakota and stopped. The old man was aware of the move and he was suddenly uneasy and had to force himself to face ahead. Farnell's face told him nothing.

"I'm just an old, old man," Dakota said, "an' I ain't good for nothin' much, anymore, but I—" He stopped speaking and rose in his saddle a little as a bullet entered his spine and Slim's gun went off, almost together. Dakota fell, slowly at first, then plunged headlong to the ground.

Farnell put his horse through the creek and hauled it in beside Dakota, looking down at the motionless body.

"Why'n hell did you do that?" he asked without concern.

"Like he's always sayin', he's an old man and not good for much. Anyway he talks a lot."

Farnell grinned at Slim. "Now tell me the real reason you killed him."

"Otis is makin' all the money," Slim complained. "He's the one havin' all the fun and gettin' five hundred dollars a head every time he puts one away."

"We'll all come out about even," Farnell said and dismounted, pushing his hat on the back of his head. "What we gonna do with Dakota? We can't leave the body lyin' here."

"There's a cutbank off the trail a piece," Slim said. "We can drag him in there and then push the bank down on top o' him. That ought to do it."

"Well, all right," Farnell agreed. "Get off your damn horse and let's get busy."

Slim stood looking at Dakota's near-thoroughbred horse. "There's a damn good-lookin' animal," he said. "What'll we do with it?"

"Can't turn it loose," Farnell said. "If it turned up at the ranch, which it will if we turn it loose, there'll be explainin' I'm not ready for."

"Hasn't got a brand," Slim said reflectively. "Ol' Dakota never did give up his ol' ways. Wouldn't ride a branded hoss." He snorted in disgust. "I'll sell him to one a them sheepherders." He went to Dakota's horse and began unsaddling the animal.

"Let's get rid of Dakota first," Farnell said.

Slim flung the saddle to the ground and went to Dakota, bent down and grasped him under his arms. Farnell lifted Dakota's legs and they carried him off through the brush toward the overhang of rock and dirt protruding over what in ancient times had been a deep creek about ten feet wide. They wedged Dakota in under the overhang and Slim went foraging for a piece of wood to loosen the dirt and rocks.

"I'll get his saddle," Farnell said. "Don't cover him up till I get his saddle."

Slim sat down in the shade of a mountain oak and relaxed, watching Farnell stride away toward the horses. Slim didn't like being alone, so he got to his feet and tramped through the brush to the seldom-used wagon road.

He came on Farnell as the latter was unbuckling the straps on Dakota's saddlebags. "I want to see what old man Boynton's always sending off," he explained, as he withdrew the brown-paper-wrapped package from the saddlebags.

Farnell got out his knife, opened a blade, sliced through the binding twine, and ripped off the paper. He stared in disbelief at the neat stacks of twenty-dollar bills, all crisp and new.

"What the hell do you think of that?" he asked, letting out a sighing gust of wind.

Slim kneeled and reached out a hand to lift a packet of bills from the box, rifling them like a deck of cards. "I never seen so goddam much money in my life!" he said hoarsely. "Where'd all this come from? An' how much more is they?"

"Not from raisin' beef," Farnell said. He shot a look at Slim. "We work this right we can both get well, never have to work another day in our life. Boynton been sending these packages out for long as we been here. Must be plenty more where this come from."

"How 'bout that feller—"

"Oh, we'll do his job for him, all right. I'd do it for nothin' just to get at that damn saddle tramp. But what we do for Raven won't interfere with us doin' for ourselves. We gotta get the rest of it, no matter what."

"What'll we do with this till we're ready to ride outta here?" Slim asked with a happy lilt to his voice.

"We'll split it right down the middle."

"What about Raven?"

Farnell shook his head. "This is between me and you," he said.

"How'll we get what's left of the money?"

Farnell looked at him contemptuously. "Take it, Slim, just take it. It'll be easy—an old man, a blind girl—yeah, and an old, old servant."

"If Coppers slips away, it won't be easy, Lute."

"He won't slip away," Farnell said positively.

CHAPTER SEVENTEEN

Coppers had run it all through his mind while riding from the Slash B to the Bennion place. He accomplished little more than to bring a dull ache to his skull.

While his mind had accumulated more bits and pieces of information than he could handle, physically he was filled with energy, impatient to get on with it. He suspected his feeling of well-being came from the fistfight with Farnell. That violence released something that had to break out or else.

He came down the long slope to the Box MB and took the shortcut. The friendly hound came to welcome him as it had before, wagging its tail and barking without malice.

"Hi ya, Hector," he said and the hound followed him around the house and watched as Coppers dismounted and tied in. Sal came from the house, smiling shyly at him, inviting him in.

Down by the barn, Coppers could see Humpy working on the stagecoach. "Humpy going to town today?" Coppers asked.

She nodded. "He's taking guests in to Laramie and bringing others back. Would you care for a cup of coffee?"

"Sure would," Coppers said and, climbing the steps, followed her into the house.

"Drink it in the kitchen," she said, "so's I can get on with dinner."

"Where's Mel?" he asked, dropping his hat on the floor and seating himself at an oilcloth-covered table in the middle of the room. Pots simmered on the big range and savory smells filled the air.

She brought a cup and saucer and placed it on the table. "You didn't know about Doctor Jasper?"

Coppers shook his head.

"No, you wouldn't know. Doc was killed the night Aletha was taken—oh, oh, I'm not supposed to say that, am I?"

"Doc Jaspers killed?" Coppers stared.

She went to the stove and lifted a big enameled coffee pot, brought it to the table, and poured coffee into his cup. She stood there, holding the pot. "It was awful, really bad. We didn't discover him till daylight yesterday, when one of the boys went in the dispensary to get something. Doc had been shot in the back and it must have happened during the big commotion, when all those horses were stampeding and people shooting—"

One more dead man, Coppers thought with a feeling almost of defeat. He'd formed an immediate liking for Doctor Jasper. He'd spent a few hours with the vet and that brief contact with Coppers had put a curse on him, as it had others, most of whom he'd met only briefly. Yet, he'd never caught a glimpse of the stalking killer. Worse yet, he had not been aware that he was being trailed. In all these shootings, Coppers had been spared. Why?

"—he was such a good man." Sal Bennion returned the coffee pot to the stove and returned to the table to take a chair across from Coppers.

Coppers laced his coffee with canned milk and spooned in sugar, stirring it thoughtfully.

"Mel's gone with the body to Rock River; that's where Doc come from originally. Mel won't be back till tomorrow sometime. I do declare!"

"Doc have any enemies around here?"

She shook her head. "He was the sweetest man on earth, Mr. Coppers. Everybody thought just the world of him." She used her apron to wipe a tear from her eye. "We'll all miss him so much, especially Tommie. Doc was always telling Tommie stories; he spent so much time with him when Mel was gone and Tommie followed him around. Doc had so much patience." She got up and went to the stove, uncovered a pot and stirred it, replaced the lid and came back to Coppers.

Lifting her skirt slightly she seated herself, resting her chin on her folded hands. "One of our guests, Mr. Donel, from Washington, D.C., was asking about you."

"I talked to him," Coppers said shortly.

"He woke us up at daylight, demanding to be taken back to Laramie. Grady told him he'd have to wait till the stage went in but he wouldn't listen. Made so much racket, Grady finally loaned him a horse and buggy and away he went."

Coppers took some pleasure in that thought, finished his coffee and stood up. "I've got to be moving," he said. "Thanks for the coffee."

"Any time," she said, following him to the door. "Come again, Dave."

Coppers walked slowly toward the barn, passing Humpy at work on the stage. Coppers raised a hand in greeting. The small man merely nodded and kept on with his work.

Walking through the barn, Coppers opened the door into the small corral and called Farah. She tossed her head from side to side, looking at him with ears tilted forward. Like many Arabians she was small and trim and he wondered at her ability to carry his weight. He'd take it slow and easy, he decided, and rest her often even though he was anxious to check the area above Horsehead Crossing to see if he could intercept Henry Eggert.

After saddling the mare, Coppers walked to where Humpy worked on the stage. "How soon you figure to leave?"

"Soon's I get the horses hitched and the dudes ready to go," he said shortly. He was not a man inclined to talk much.

The mare swung her head and whickered. Coppers turned to stare at an oncoming group of riders.

Humpy straightened as much as he could, muttering, "Scott Tyrell!"

Four horsemen continued past the shortcut and crossed the creek, passing the ranch house and drawing up beside the stage.

A huge square man riding a heavy, big-footed black gelding stared down at Coppers. He ran his hand down his thick black beard and spoke in a low, grating voice: "You're the man brought in the body o' Gil Tatum?" he asked.

Coppers nodded.

"You want a job?"

"Riding or fighting?"

"Some of one, more of t'other."

"I've got a job."

"On the Slash B?" he grunted. "Can't be much of a job."

"It'll do until a better one shows up."

"If you won't work for me, let me tell you something—don't go hiring out to Will Talbot. That'd be the quickest way to big trouble I know about."

"Old men are pretty good at giving advice," Coppers said.

Tyrell flushed. "What the hell does that mean?" he blustered. He patted his shirt pocket and found a cigar. He lighted it and puffed deeply, pursing his lips to emit a few small quick smoke rings. "Anybody with a lick of sense listens to good counsel."

"Let me give you some, then," Coppers said. "Stop your damn war. Nobody wins or loses."

"He started it and by damn I'll finish it."

"I rode by the sheep camp. Your man did a good job on the herders. Both dead. I got there just in time to cut the dogs loose or they'd have been burned alive."

Tyrell spat out a tobacco leaf. "Damn sheep dogs, just like the herders, can't tell the difference. Means nothin' to me." He lifted his reins, gave a look around at his hard-bitten crew and nodded. "Don't take sides," he threw over his shoulder. "You don't work for me, you don't work for Talbot."

Looking after them, Humpy said, "Gonna be hell to pay. Talbot's men headed that way just 'fore you rode in."

"They're after a fight?"

"You could say that. Well, no skin off my nose." He went back to his work.

The wind blew soft and warm off Medicine Bow Range from Laramie Peak, swept over the rounded hills and into the valleys, stirring the brush and lifting dust devils in open spaces. Coppers breathed deeply of the scent of pine and spruce and sage and had to hold in the frisky mare as she wanted to run.

He checked his rifle as he rode. Keeping the mare at a slow walk despite her eagerness to run, he found the dim trail wound through cottonwoods along the creek bottoms, with tall slim pine trees on the hills on both sides. Brush grew so thick that his legs scraped against the tough branches. Now and then he had to lean low in the saddle to avoid an overhanging limb of a higher clump of brush. He came into a small clearing and stopped the mare to listen. He could hear nothing but the horse breathing and the strident call of a crow in the far distance. He urged the mare into motion again, keeping her to a walk. He could see better ahead now as the trees thinned out. He began to suspect that Henry Eggert had not taken a chance on Gard's carrying the ransom note to Boynton, waiting for the signal, and then coming on to the rendezvous. His lack of sure knowledge irritated him, and the same old thoughts going around and around in his head irritated him even more.

A smear of smoke hovering above a clump of cottonwoods brought him up short as he reined in the mare. He stared at the smoke for a moment and then looked all around before dismounting. He tied the mare to a clump of brush off the trail. Carrying his rifle at ready he went ahead on foot, walking slowly, stopping often to look around, including to his rear.

He stopped and squatted suddenly as he caught sight of Eggert's camp. The man's fire was smoldering, almost dead, and he was reclining nearby, his hat over his face. Eggert's horse on a lariat grazed nearby, in a small meadow beyond the camp.

Coppers edged noiselessly over the edge of the creek bank and into the water which ran placid a short stretch. He felt cold water enter breaks in his old boots as he advanced up the narrow watercourse, screened by the bank of the creek. When he was opposite Eggert's camp he raised up, leveling the rifle.

Eggert sat upright but made no move for a weapon. His rifle lay on the ground beside him. He'd removed his gunbelt and it lay within reach on top of his rifle. "I ain't makin' a play," he said. His reddish whiskers streaked with white deepened the blue of his eyes in his leathery square face. He was approaching or past middle age, Coppers guessed, and mild appearing. There was a frying pan and a smoke-blackened can for coffee beside the smoldering ashes of the campfire. "Sit an' have a cup o' coffee," Henry Eggert invited.

"Been here long?" Coppers asked politely.

"Day or so, more or less. You passin' through?"

"I'm hanging around hereabouts."

"Ah, you're not with Tyrell or Talbot?"

"No."

"You're headin' right into 'em," Eggert said, waving his hand up the canyon. "They're on opposite sides this little canyon and I been watchin' 'em since Tyrell got here. He's been trackin' Talbot's gang and now they're just about ready to go at it again."

"You saw them?"

Eggert pointed above. "From that high ridge up there you can see a long way off. I heard their racket and went up for a look. Seems they're not sure 'bout who is who or else they'd a started shootin' awready. Now, when I—" He ducked as bullets ripped into the campfire knocking over the coffee can, and the thunder of rifles shattered the silence.

Coppers and Eggert took cover as one in the creek bed.

"Sonofabitch, they think we're them," Eggert remarked. "Last bit o' coffee I had was in that can." Cupping his hands to his mouth he shouted, "We ain't cattle or sheep, boys!" A hail of lead swept down over them. Eggert crouched under the bank, looking at Coppers. "Think they heard me?"

Coppers said, "They heard you and don't believe you."

After that initial volley, the firing dwindled to a lone shot now and then. The lead slugs landed in the opposite bank with a thunking sound. One slug glanced off a rock and whined off into space.

Coppers caught sight of movement above, raised his rifle, and fired in one easy motion. A yell came down to them.

"By God, you got one," Eggert said with satisfaction. "Wisht I had my guns."

"Go get them," Coppers said. "I'll cover you."

"Get another shell or two in your rifle first," Eggert said.

Coppers complied, inserting two brass cartridges in the magazine of his Winchester. "It's got all it'll hold now."

Eggert crawled up to the lip of the grassy bank and peered over, looking up at the ridge on either side. "All right, let 'er rip," he said, and scuttled up to the grassy bank while Coppers set up a steady firing at both factions facing one another on the ridges separated by the shallow canyon.

Eggert snatched up his weapons and raced back to the creek and jumped down, splashing water on Coppers. "Got 'em," he said triumphantly, buckling on his pistol belt and levering a shell into the firing chamber of his Winchester.

"All right, you bastids," he said. "You ast for it." He raised his rifle and fired and another yell came floating down to them. "I hit that rock up there and just stung him," Eggert remarked. "They keepin' better hid than they was." He fired again and both groups above began pouring shots into the creek bed. They were firing blind, Coppers guessed, because both he and Eggert were well-protected by the creek bank.

The shooting went on, running randomly along the tops of both ridges. Coppers was reminded of the Spanish guns at San Juan during that slow walk to the top with men falling all around. He pushed all this from his mind to concentrate on the present.

Coppers glanced at Eggert and saw him scanning the ridge to their right. When Eggert sensed his stare and turned his head, Coppers nodded. "I'm going up the creek a piece," he said. "Long as we're here we might as well try to stop this fighting."

"You can try to stop it if you want," Eggert said. "I'm just tryin' to stay alive."

Coppers grinned at him and went up the creek, bent from the waist, protected by the brushy bank, the brush having replaced the grassy area where Eggert camped. A fish darted away ahead of him; big trout, he thought. He stopped, listening for sound between the occasional shots, accompanied by a high-pitched yell now and then, or a curse.

Coppers continued, reached a turn in the creek, and stopped to listen again. He swiveled his head around and saw the man above and behind Eggert taking aim with a rifle. He threw up his rifle and fired and the man fell forward. Eggert looked over his shoulder and then faced Coppers, raising his rifle and waving it. Coppers answered the signal and continued up the creek. He got around the turn and saw at one glance the three men lying in the shelter of a cluster of rocks.

Coppers thumbed back the hammer of his Winchester and squatted until his eyes were level with the creek bank. He sighted in on the rocks and fired a shot which sprayed broken rock on the three men. He fired again as the men tried to get closer to the ground. "Next time it'll be right at you. Throw your guns out."

The man nearest Coppers rolled over levering his Winchester, but Coppers' quick bullet stopped all his motion. He jerked once under the impact of the bullet and lay still. The other two scrambled on their hands and knees out of sight into the rock cluster, leaving their rifles behind. Off to his left, on the opposite ridge, two hidden riflemen set up a steady firing that cut all around him. He retreated the way he'd come and failed to see any target to shoot at.

He came round a turn in the creek and stopped, listening to the wild, confused shouts that came up from what he thought was the sheepman side of the conflict. The shooting had died away. He heard the pound of hard-running horses, a sound that quickly faded, leaving a heavy silence in the canyon.

He climbed to the top of the ridge and found three dead men, none of whom he'd seen before, all strangers to him. He scouted briefly and then crossed the canyon and climbed the other side. The sheep faction had suffered two deaths. The heavy silence continued to hold. Not even the crows or jays argued back and forth as they usually did.

He went down the slope with long strides and on reaching the bottom turned toward Eggert's camp. In less than five minutes he broke out of the brush cover and into the clear grassy area where Eggert had pitched his camp.

Eggert and his horse were gone.

CHAPTER EIGHTEEN

Coppers neared the Slash B after nightfall, somewhere around nine o'clock. Trotting Farah downgrade, he felt her quicken her pace as she sensed the nearness of the home corral, water, and feed.

The castle windows on the ground were lighted. Yellow squares of dusty glass indicated the bunkhouse was occupied. Strains of organ music reached Coppers as he neared the castle, and with the achingly sweet sounds of the music came a sudden release of tension.

He slacked his reins and Farah obediently moved toward the barn. He stepped to the ground, unsaddled the mare, and rubbed her down. He lit the lantern and hung it on a nail inside the barn. He led Farah back to a box stall and placed a generous measure of oats in the feed bin and threw hay down from the loft into the manger. He returned to the entry, extinguished the lantern, and walked through the night to the back door of the castle. Inside he could hear the clatter of dishes as Wash cleaned up from the evening meal. The organ music was more muted here in the rear area of the castle.

He tapped on the back door and opened it and went inside as Wash peered out from the kitchen door into the darkened, enclosed back porch.

"That you, Mista Coppers, suh?" Wash asked in a shaky and fearful voice.

"Yes." He came soft-footed toward the open door and Wash backed away quickly. "I'm starved. Anything left over from supper?"

"Yea, suh, Mista Coppers. You sit right down there at the table an' I fixes you a bite, got some good stew still in the warmer."

Coppers crossed the room, dropped his hat on the floor beside the chair, and sat down, folding his hands on the red-and-white tablecloth.

In almost no time at all, Wash placed a plate of stew and a mound of golden flaky biscuits in front of Coppers. Coppers ate quickly and without wasted motion while Wash brought him a cup of coffee before resuming his kitchen chores.

"Who's in the bunkhouse?" Coppers asked.

"Mista Farnell, Mista Slim."

"Mr. Boynton still up?"

Wash nodded. "Yas, suh, he sho' is."

"Tell him I want to talk to him," Coppers said, taking out his sack of tobacco and starting the fashioning of a cigarette.

Wash stared at him apprehensively.

"Do you understand what I said?" Coppers asked sharply.

"Yas, suh, I sho' do. I go get Mr. Boynton." He backed across the room to the inside door and on reaching it turned quickly and disappeared.

Coppers was finishing his cigarette when Wash wheeled Boynton into the kitchen. The old man nodded silently at Coppers, his eyes bright and alert. Coppers crossed his knife and fork on his plate and nodded Wash out of the room.

Wash left the room reluctantly, casting glances first at Boynton who paid him no mind and Coppers who gave him a stern look.

Boynton, stroking his goatee, eyed Coppers warily. "Yes, Mr. Coppers," he said evenly.

Coppers took out a sack of tobacco. "Mind if I smoke?"

"Not at all. Would you prefer a cigar?"

Coppers shook his head, a cigarette already taking shape beneath his quick fingers. He licked the paper in place and placed the cigarette in his mouth and lighted a match on his thumbnail and put it to the twisted end of the cigarette. "I must apologize, first, for coming to you under false colors."

Boynton dropped his hand to the armrest of his wheelchair. "False colors?"

Coppers nodded. He rose and walked around Boynton and returned to the table and sat on its edge. "I work for the Agency—"

"Secret Service?"

"Yes. You must know why I'm here."

"I've no idea, sir," Boynton said stiffly. "Not the faintest."

"I believe you do have more than just an idea, Mr. Boynton," Coppers said gently. He took out the wrinkled, creased ransom note, leaned forward and offered it to Boynton. "Look at this, sir. You're taking your granddaughter into danger, Mr. Boynton. I'm sure you'd not want that."

Boynton read the ransom demands, his face crumpling, his shoulders sagging. "They—they kidnaped Aletha? Why wasn't I told?"

"It didn't suit my purpose to tell you," Coppers said. "I never tell anyone any more than I have to."

"How do I know you're not in this game yourself?"

Coppers shrugged. "You'll have to trust me, sir."

"I'm afraid that's impossible—now."

"Listen to me. I'm a Secret Service agent. Make no mistake about that. I've no identification because I came here incognito to do my work in secret."

Boynton kept his eyes steadily on Coppers' face.

"I can tell you one thing, though. Your man in Denver, Professor Lemuel P. Taylor, whom you know well, is at this moment in Laramie or Arapaho—or en route there. I suspect that the so-called professor is not satisfied with his percentage. He wants to take it all. He has some pretty bad actors working for him. I'm not sure just how many there are. The longer you stall the greater the danger to Aletha—and to yourself."

As Coppers talked in a low, earnest, convincing voice, Boynton pressed his thin transparent hands to his face. When Coppers' voice stopped, silence came to the kitchen, except for the soft strains of the organ in the parlor. Boynton dropped his hands and raised a haggard face to Coppers. His eyes were wet with tears.

"Washington, come here, please," Boynton called.

Wash must have been waiting outside the door. He entered at once and walked swiftly to Boynton's side. "What de matter, suh?" he asked, glowering at Coppers.

"Bring me a glass of brandy, Washington," Boynton said. He looked up at Coppers. "Would you care to join me, sir?"

"No, thank you."

Boynton nodded to Washington and the black man disappeared. The organ had stopped. Silence prevailed until Washington returned with a crystal goblet filled with dark amber liquid on a tray. He held the tray before Boynton, and the old man groped for it, raised the glass to his lips, and gulped half of it in one swallow. He nodded Washington away.

"Brandy is for sipping," he said apologetically. "I must confess that I've experienced nightmares. What I've done hasn't rested easy on my conscience."

"I'm sure it has not."

"When I retired from Treasury everything seemed so bright, so promising," Boynton said. "I had enough money to purchase this place. There was a pension that would pay expenses, plus a little in investments here and there. Then everything went bad, my pension, investments, everything. I stood to lose all I'd invested in the Slash B—and all else, everything I owned.

"I came out here before Aletha; she remained behind with friends in Virginia. I looked the property over very carefully. The house was a shambles, not fit for a dog to live in. I was exploring an old root cellar under the house when I found the money. Just as it was taken from the train in the robbery twenty or so years ago. I knew immediately what had happened. It was money being shipped back East to be destroyed because of a flaw."

"It lacked the signature of the U. S. Treasurer," Coppers said.

Boynton looked at him in surprise. "Yes. Of course you would know." He sat silent for a moment and then continued: "I had hired a local workman to build a new place. I discharged him when I found the money, brought in a group of foreign workmen and had them build the house to my specifications, which included a workshop where the old root cellar had been. I worked there to rectify the Bureau of Engraving's error. I only worked on enough to keep a steady cash flow. I've disposed of less than two hundred thousand dollars. The remainder is in a safe downstairs in my workshop.

"I had to have help to dispose of the money. I contacted the son of an old, old friend of mine. Lemuel was never much account but he was a likable lad, everybody's friend. He agreed to help me."

"What percentage did he get?"

"Fifteen percent. He wanted more but I talked him down. He was glad to get it in the end."

"At first, maybe," Coppers said. "Then greed got the best of him. He wanted all of it."

"He was like a member of my family," Boynton protested. "Aletha liked him—"

"Let's put away this kind of talk," Coppers said roughly. What I'm trying to do, he told himself, is figure out some way to get the money on its way to Washington, D.C., and put Aletha in a safe place until this is all settled. There was no question in his mind that the wolves, coyotes, and buzzards circling the Slash B would descend like a plague.

A noise at the back door brought him around sharply.

Deputy Shug Kruger stood in the doorway with a double-barreled, sawed-off shotgun aimed at him. Both hammers were back.

"She's loaded with double-ought buckshot," Kruger said steadily as he stared at Coppers. Two faces peered over Kruger's shoulder and light glinted on their handguns.

"What's up?" Coppers asked in a mild voice.

"What's up feller," Kruger said with enormous satisfaction, "is that I arrest you in the name of the law." He stepped inside the door and sidestepped to reveal two posse members. Sounds of horses outside indicated there were more of them. "Get his gun, boys, and make sure he don't have a hideaway."

"What's the charge?" Coppers asked in the same tone of voice.

"We got a lot o' them," Kruger said. "Let's start with this one—Butch Cassidy!"

Chief of Secret Service Charles Effington sat in the anteroom of the Oval Office morosely uncomfortable. He had his legs crossed and his elbows rested on the arms of the uncomfortable chair which allowed him to steeple his fingers and to keep from drumming them nervously.

A soft-footed secretary approached and tilted his head, whispering, "The President will see you now, Chief Effington."

Effington sprang to his feet, almost trampling the heels of the secretary. He cautioned himself, forced himself to walk slowly, if not confidently, to a meeting he'd rather not attend. Effington had abandoned all attempts to guess what this presidential summons meant.

The President was seated at his desk, staring at a single sheet of paper in front of him. The desk was clear except for that one sheet of paper which was fully covered with writing.

"Please be seated," the President said, and Effington could clearly hear the clack of the big white teeth as Roosevelt bit off his words.

My God, thought Effington, he's mad about something. He sat on the edge of the chair conveniently near the President's desk. He stole a look at the bronzed man sitting there like a statue, his eyes unblinking behind the pince-nez glasses, his moustache bristling. He raised his eyes and something in that glance chilled Effington through and through.

Over Roosevelt's shoulder Effington could see the Remington statuette presented to Roosevelt by his men on the day the Rough Riders disbanded on Long Island.

"There are all kinds of ties," Roosevelt said, enunciating each word distinctly and clacking his teeth. "Childhood friends, family ties, school ties, and so on. When you go to war with a man, you build a special tie with him. Men under arms! That's the strongest ever. My boys—the Rough Riders and I didn't choose the name—were ready to give up their lives at an instant's notice for their country—and for me. That makes for a lifelong relationship, one I respect, even revere. I told my boys on that day that I'd always cherish them, no matter the fortunes of their lives or my own. By George, I meant it then and I mean it now."

"Yes, sir," Effington murmured. "I was too young for the Civil War and too old for the Spanish one."

Roosevelt gave him another of those spine-chilling glances.

"I shook the hand of every one of those men that day," Roosevelt continued. "I'll never forget a single one of them. Never!"

Chief Effington felt humble in the aura created by Roosevelt's passion. There was no doubting his sincerity even if Effington had heard strange stories of this remarkable man.

"One in particular," he said, pulling the paper in front of him closer and looking at it. "David Coppers. Does the name mean anything to you, Chief?"

"Yes, sir," Effington said, nodding, his throat dry. "One of my operatives."

"What is the story behind his assignment in Wyoming?"

Chief Effington swallowed with difficulty. "I have the barest outline of the detail, sir. My next in command handled all the matters of that particular case."

"You should have brought your next in command with you."

"I'm sorry, sir, but he—he's on special assignment himself."

"What are the circumstances?"

Effington tried to think but found his thought process in a state of disorder. "Skiles—my assistant—is en route to Wyoming to try to solve a problem that has arisen in connection with the case in question—"

"Please do not give me bureaucratic claptrap," Roosevelt said sternly, his teeth snapping shut on each word with a sound that penetrated all corners of the room.

"Sir, I do not have all the facts," Effington said in desperation.

"Inform me of those you do have."

"My assistant planned the operation, to recover bank notes taken in a train robbery, fifteen or twenty years ago. He recommended Coppers for the mission because Coppers was born in Wyoming Territory but had been away long enough that he wouldn't be recognized. I believe I must regretfully say no more about this, pending a consultation with Mr. Skiles."

"I have a letter here from a citizen," Roosevelt said, "which I will not read to you, but in essence states that Coppers was ill-prepared to venture forth on this mission. There are other serious accusations. I must warn you, Chief Effington, if anything untoward happens to Coppers, I'll hold you personally responsible. Is that sufficiently clear?"

"Yes, sir," Effington said. "Who wrote the letter?" Not that it matters he told himself glumly.

Roosevelt stared coldly at him. "You have a right to know," he said. He glanced at the letter as if for verification. "A Mrs. Ida Mae Courtney." He turned the paper over with a slap of his hand. "That's all, Chief."

Effington rose and bowed. "Thank you, sir," Effington said, preparing to move toward the door.

"Do not go away, Chief, not until I express my appreciation

for the very fine work you did in Toronto during our war with Spain. You did a splendid job containing the spy ring. I want you to know your contribution has not been forgotten by any means."

"Thank you, Mr. President," Effington said, his growing admiration for Roosevelt suddenly increasing without restraint. "Thank you very much!"

"Good!" The President rose and Effington stiffened into attention. The President reached across his desk and shook hands with Effington. "Be prepared to travel on short notice," he said tersely and, with a nod, dismissed Effington.

CHAPTER NINETEEN

Coppers sat motionless in his chair, staring at Kruger. Did the man remember him from their brush on the train west in the incident involving Sal Bennion? Kruger had been drunk that night. Now he was alert and excitement flushed his face and brightened his eyes.

"Pinky, you get his gun," Kruger directed. "Don't get twixt him and this scattergun."

Pinky, a cowboy with freckled pink skin and reddish hair and a pouting mouth, stepped gingerly along the wall and approached Coppers from the rear.

"You must be out of your mind," Coppers said.

Kruger nodded, half-smiling. "From pure joy," he said. "Never dreamed I'd lay hands on the notorious Butch Cassidy."

"You haven't," Coppers said. "From what I hear, Cassidy was killed in some South American country."

"All planted," Kruger said. He opened the flap on his shirt pocket and extracted a fold of paper. "Take a look at this, fella, and then tell me you ain't Butch Cassidy." He tossed the paper on the table before Coppers.

Pinky gingerly extracted Coppers' Colt from its holster and looked at it before sticking it in the waistband of his pants.

"Make sure he ain't got another gun on him," Kruger warned.

Coppers sat motionless as Pinky patted him under his arms and ran his hands up and down his leg. When Pinky moved away Coppers opened the paper, unfolding and pressing out the creases, to find a wanted poster of the usual kind found in post offices and courthouses across the land. The picture on the poster was an unmistakable likeness of Coppers, rendered by some unknown artist whose initials were M.S.

"Where'd you get this?" Coppers asked.

"Same place I get most o' them," Kruger said. "Through the mail."

"I believe Mr. Boynton can swear to you I'm not Butch Cassidy," Coppers said, swinging his head to look at Boynton.

Boynton sat alertly, a gleam in his eye the only sign of emotion. Boynton nodded solemnly. "Mr. Coppers is not Butch Cassidy," he said succinctly.

Kruger snorted his disbelief. "Just like that, hey? You sayin' so don't make it true. This is what counts." He reached out and yanked the wanted poster from Coppers' hand and stuffed it back into his shirt pocket. "That—and other stuff."

"What other stuff?"

"Show him, Pinky," Kruger said.

Pinky pulled a canvas money sack from inside his shirt and held it up for all to see. The printing on the canvas sack read: STOCKMAN'S BANK OF WYOMING. "We got this out from under your bunk right in the Slash B bunkhouse. Bank held up yesterday over Laramie way by two men. Only a few hundred dollars in this sack but more than sixteen thousand took in the bank holdup."

"I don't know a thing about that," Coppers said.

Kruger simulated a pained expression. "That's what they all say, boy," he said wearily. "We got you cold turkey, man, so why don't you come clean?"

"Yeah, and tell us where the rest o' the money is and who your sidekick was."

"We gonna stand around yappin' all night?" one of the posse members asked. "I tore outta town not tellin' my ol' lady where I was goin'."

Kruger ignored the complaint. "You got a lot o' questions to answer, Cassidy," he said. "A heap o' killin' happened since you showed up around here. Gil Tatum for one, and pore ol' Al Hunter, you the last man to see him alive. Spud Oliver, who's no great loss for sure, but there's Doc Jasper, a finer man never lived! An' that ain't all, by a long shot. You jus' about wiped out the Tyrell and Talbot crews up above Horsehead Crossing. You workin' for both them big ikes?"

Coppers was silent. No use talking to Kruger. His mind was made up.

"You must be workin' both sides, all right. Way I hear it, you got three of Tyrell's men and two of Talbot's."

"He just might a put an end to that shenanigan single-handed," Pinky observed. "Ones still alive done pulled up stakes and cleared out."

"What—what is wrong?" called a clear voice holding a note of alarm, and all of them swiveled their heads around to stare at Aletha Boynton. Washington stood behind her with an old muzzle-loading shotgun clutched in his two hands.

Deputy Kruger lifted his hat. "Ma'am," he said, "I'm takin' this feller in custody. Turns out he's the notorious Butch Cassidy, wanted in a number of states for just about every crime on the books. Fifty thousand dollars reward for his capture. Dead or alive."

"Dave?"

Coppers stood up and cleared his throat.

She walked swiftly to his side and placed her hand on his arm. "He simply couldn't be Cassidy," she declared. "From all I've heard Cassidy was fifteen or twenty years older than Dave."

"Well, maybe. We'll find out. But there's that bank robbery charge, too."

"He couldn't have had anything to do with that," Aletha protested. "He has been here all the time."

"That's not how Lute, er, another witness tells it."

"I know he couldn't be guilty," Aletha politely objected. "He's not that kind of man."

"How long you known him, Miss Aletha?" Kruger asked.

"He—he helped me when a cougar attacked—actually I've not known him long, Deputy, in time that is; but a person doesn't need a lot of time to tell another's character. You should know that."

"If you could see him you'd change your tune."

"I—I have s—seen him," Aletha said shakily, and then rushed on, her words tumbling out: "With what I have to see, with my —my heart, my ears, my hands—" She stopped speaking, confused, her face coloring.

Despite all that was happening, Coppers felt his spirit lift as he looked at her. His gaze hardened and shifted to Kruger. "Who tipped you off?" Coppers asked.

"I'm not sayin' right now," Kruger responded shortly and turned his back on Coppers. "I know you convinced yourself, Miss Aletha, an' you think you're right. But I got to take him in. Let's get movin', boys. Pinky, saddle him a horse."

"The buckskin is mine," Coppers said, and Aletha's low cry of pain lingered in the room.

"The buckskin is saddled and I'm waitin'," a voice called from outside. "We ready to go when you are, Shug."

A day and night in the cramped cell in the Arapaho jail left Coppers caged, restless, miserable. The jail, a low, squat rock building behind the building housing the city government, was barren except for a bunk built of peeled pine poles with a straw tick, a slop pail, and a tin bucket of water.

Coppers paced the narrow confines, remembering the triumphant gleam in Boynton's eyes when Deputy Kruger led him out of the castle, handcuffed him to the saddle horn after he was mounted. During the ride into Arapaho, Coppers tried to persuade Kruger to leave a couple of men on guard at the Slash B. Kruger stubbornly refused to listen.

Coppers couldn't keep his mind off what might be happening at the Slash B. Farnell and Slim were moving in to take the booty, and Coppers could only guess at how many other scavengers were directly involved in the grab for the money.

He wondered how Farnell would conduct himself with Aletha. Farnell appeared to be in love with Aletha, but it did not seem to Coppers to be the kind of love a decent man has for a respectable woman. He asked himself if Farnell would amuse himself with Aletha if the opportunity presented itself and found no answer, only a maddening frustration and fury.

Then, too, there was old Washington's quite obvious fear of Farnell. That told Coppers a lot about Farnell. He suspected that Aletha, and perhaps her grandfather too, had not the slightest idea of Farnell's real character.

Coppers' view of the main street of Arapaho was limited from the window of his jail cell. He could see the stage station, next to the hotel, but as there were only two stages a week there wasn't much activity in that part of town. Men clustered in front of the Wild Belle and moved in and out aimlessly. He knew this from the sounds rather than sight. The Wild Belle was on the opposite side of the street and at times he got confused sounds mixed with those from the Saloon which was on the same side of the street as the jail but not visible to him.

Twice a day, Kruger came in with his double-barreled shotgun cocked and aimed through the bars at Coppers while an aged jailer unlocked the door and placed a tray of food inside the cell while looking wall-eyed at Coppers. This done, he retreated hastily through the door, slammed it shut, and locked the door with an enormous key. The food came from the hotel and consisted of leftovers all plopped together on a tin tray. It didn't matter because Coppers' appetite had left him.

On the morning of the second day, the sheriff entered the cellblock holding his shotgun in one hand and his other hand on Aletha's elbow.

Coppers jumped to his feet, staring in disbelief. Slowly his sudden start subsided and he looked at Aletha. She carried a cloth-covered basket on her arm.

The sheriff unlocked Coppers' cell door and pushed it open with his foot. He had his shotgun trained on Coppers.

"Sorry, ma'am," he said apologetically. "I gotta see what's in your basket."

She laughed gaily as she removed the linen cover, revealing the contents.

Kruger leaned over inspecting the contents of the basket. "Guess that looks all right," he said, straightening.

"Fried chicken," she said, replacing the cover deftly. "And fried apple pies, an old southern delicacy. I made them myself—with Washington's help, of course."

"They're bound to be good then," Deputy Kruger said gallantly as he waited for her to enter the cell. When she was inside the cell, he locked the door, uncocked his shotgun, and gusted a sigh. "Can't let you stay long," he warned as he departed.

Aletha stood there and Coppers came to her and took the basket from her and placed it on his bunk. He came back to her and took her hands, gripping them in his own.

She trembled slightly. "Ah, Dave," she said, "I'm so sorry this happened to you."

He felt the warmth of her hands and their answering pressure.

It seemed to him that suddenly the world was a brighter place.

"How are things at the Slash B?"

"Quiet. Very quiet."

"Any strangers around the place?"

She shook her head wonderingly. "No. Why do you ask?"

He forced a laugh. "Perilous times, these. I'd advise you to stay indoors and keep everything locked."

Her smile faded. "What is threatening us, Dave? Surely you can confide in me."

"I'm not sure," he said almost despairingly. "I wish I knew and I'd gladly tell you. I'd give anything in the world to make sure you're not hurt."

"You're talking just like Grandfather," she said. "He wants me to leave immediately and go back East for the eye operation. That's all he talks about lately."

"Do it," Coppers urged. "Do it now. Don't go back to the Slash B, Aletha. I believe you'd not be safe there."

"If I'm not safe neither is Grandfather. I can't leave now, with all this going on. I can't desert now that we're in rough times. And I do want to know that you'll be free of all these silly charges and Kruger will release you."

"It's not that simple," Coppers said. "There's so much going on I don't know about. Makes me feel helpless even when I'm not locked up."

"You'll be vindicated," Aletha said firmly. "I'll do all I can, Dave, to help you. But you'll have to tell me what I must do to help."

"Get word to Dakota I want to see him." Coppers had a notion that Dakota was swinging away from Farnell. There was friction in the trio and Coppers could see signs of Dakota's changing attitude toward Farnell. The old man knew Butch Cassidy and if it came to a showdown he, Coppers, might be able to get Dakota to testify that he was not Butch Cassidy. The bank robbery charge was something else.

Aletha was frowning. "Lute Farnell told me that Dakota quit and rode away," Aletha said. "He was such a nice old man. I thought he was content on the Slash B, working for us."

Coppers felt an edginess rise in him. He fought off the wild feeling that would make his life a hell in this jail cell if it fully possessed him. "Most men are not content, even when they have everything good," he said.

"What did you want of Dakota?"

"Just an idea. Wasn't important. Are you going to do as I asked, that is, lock yourself in the castle—I mean the ranch house at the Slash B—and wait for word?"

"Word of what, Dave?"

She was all innocence. The old man had not confided in her, of that he was sure. "I'm not certain," he said, fully realizing that he was almost as helpless as this blind woman who attracted him more strongly than any woman he'd known.

"I've always felt very secure in my home."

"Do you realize what's going on, Aletha?" he asked.

"Only that I miss you very much! If you were free—" She broke off abruptly, silent for a moment and then continued: "Deputy Kruger won't listen to anything I say. I feel so helpless; it's maddening!"

Her worry added to his own. He didn't tell her just how worried he really was. That wouldn't help matters. The way he felt toward her he wanted to protect her, keep her safe. He knew that Kruger posted a guard around the clock. Men in Arapaho gathered, and there was dark talk among them of a quick hanging which would settle matters once and for all. In Coppers' short time in Wyoming, he had acquired a fearsome but totally undeserved reputation as a cold-blooded killer.

Aletha turned and took a few steps toward the cell door. "I—I hope I'm doing the right thing," she said, and then her chin lifted. "I believe in you, Dave. I want you to know that."

Coppers felt emotion surge up, building an unaccustomed tightness in his chest. "Knowing that helps me a lot," he said.

"I'll go now. I'll be thinking of you."

And he'd be thinking of her as he had been thinking since that first look at her on the canyon trail after the encounter with the mountain lion. It seemed that his life turned around at that particular moment.

She called out and Kruger came with his shotgun and opened the cell door. He relocked the door and silently escorted Aletha outside.

The odor of the food in the basket brought a sharp pain to

Coppers' belly. His appetite had faded when he was locked in the Arapaho jail. Now he found himself ravenously hungry. He uncovered the basket and looked it over. Cold fried chicken, golden brown, a chunk of cornbread, and fat fried pies from which apple filling oozed. He brought out a piece of chicken and began eating.

Deputy Kruger opened the outside door and came back to lean his shotgun against the bars of the adjoining cell, out of Coppers' reach. The deputy found a seat on the heels of his boots as he squatted in the corridor. He eyed the food Coppers was eating with interest.

"Have a piece of chicken," Coppers said and passed the deputy a golden-brown portion. The deputy grunted his thanks and began eating and talking around his chewing.

"I'm gettin' a little worried, feller," he announced. "Talk is there's a necktie party shapin' up—for you."

"I'd hate to see that happen," Coppers said, "seeing as how you've got the wrong man."

"Oh, I'm satisfied you're Butch, all right. Only thing I can't understand is what happened to change you into a killer. Butch didn't go for the rough stuff on a job. When he first started out, he didn't know the outlaws and time and again he'd team up with a trigger happy outlaw an' he didn't like it. Feller who pulled rough stuff when doin' a job with Butch never got another chance. Finally, Butch got Elza Lay and Harry Longabaugh, fellers just like him, didn't shoot at a wink, and he stayed with them. So far as I know Butch never killed a man. Don't know why I'm tellin' you all this, you know it better'n I do. You're him."

"You send that telegram to Washington?"

Kruger nodded. "I sent a man into Laramie with it. We ain't got no telegraph or telephone in Arapaho."

"Then soon as Washington answers you'll get the truth," Coppers said. "I'm not worried, not about myself. But I'm sure worried about those people at the Slash B ranch."

"You mean Miss Aletha?" Kruger asked slyly.

"Yes." Coppers brought out a fried pie from the basket and looked at it.

"Why don't you confess and let's end all this palaver," Kruger said. "I'm not worried about you not bein' Butch Cassidy. You tell me who helped you with that holdup and I'll say a good word for you to the prosecutor."

"The prosecutor'll never get a chance to see me," Coppers muttered. "That bunch out there drinking up a hanging will see to that."

"Maybe. I got a guard on day an' night. But I'm thinkin' about slippin' you away to Cheyenne. They got a first-class jail over there." He leered at Coppers. "Maybe you'd get Tom Horn's old cell."

Coppers looked around the small building with its four cells, stone walls, and barred windows. "Looks stout enough to me," he said.

"I hate to tell you, but this jail won't keep that bunch out when they decide to come an' get you."

Coppers bit into the apple pie and felt his teeth grate against something unyielding. He looked at the deputy who was busy gnawing on a chicken bone and hadn't heard the sound. Coppers bit around the hard object and casually dropped the pie into the basket and replaced the cloth cover. The deputy continued to chew ruminatively. Coppers relaxed.

Deputy Kruger finished the last bit of chicken and stood up, hoisting his pants. "I done made up my mind," he said sucking his teeth noisily. "We'll be leavin' here 'round midnight. I got this gut feelin' that you won't last long if I don't get you outta Arapaho. People 'round here thought a heap o' ol' Al Hunter. Want me to take that basket?"

"No. I've some food left in it."

Kruger extracted a match from his vest pocket, sharpened it with his thumbnail, and began picking his teeth. He belched. "Be ready," he said and, picking up his shotgun, strolled toward the door.

"All I have to do," Coppers said, "is put on my hat."

As soon as Kruger disappeared, Coppers removed the pie from the basket and broke it apart. He separated the pie and a metal object fell to the floor. He wiped it clean and looked at it, an eight-inch-long hacksaw blade. He couldn't keep back a chuckle at Aletha's innocence; but it had worked. He strolled to the window and looked closely at the stout iron bars. It would take a lot of time to saw through the bars with that short piece of hacksaw blade. If Kruger meant to transfer him to Cheyenne, he didn't have that much time. He sat on his bunk and then lay back, lacing his fingers together and resting his head in his hands. He studied the ceiling of rough planking, trying to dredge up some kind of decision that would eliminate the need for the hacksaw. There were four bars to each window; by taking out just one bar he might be able to squeeze through though he doubted he had even that much time. Kruger had mentioned midnight as the time for slipping away to avoid a lynch mob. The shadows falling on the cell floor told him all he needed to know: he simply didn't have time enough to saw through the bars.

Another thought hammering through all the other flashes that passed through his mind was the sense of urgency that he had to get out of this jail and back to the Slash B ranch. There was trouble building there like storm clouds over the mountains.

Well after dark, he strolled to the window and looked out into the night. A few yellow rectangles of light dotted the darkness. The street was almost deserted except for an occasional rider drifting up the street, heading for the Saloon or the Wild Belle, or a storekeeper hurrying homeward. A piano tinkled in the distance. A mule or burro brayed lustily from a nearby corral. The unending murmur of voices reached him as men talked about Arapaho's fleeting claim to fame in bringing in the most notorious outlaw of the century. Butch Cassidy rivaled and, some claimed, outshone Jesse James.

He placed the hacksaw against the rusty iron of the bar but stopped all motion when a match flared in the night a dozen feet away. It was one of the guards assigned to guard the jail night and day.

Coppers repressed an urge to swear. One rasp of that hacksaw blade would have alerted the guard. He stood there, looking out into the night, a sickness in his belly. A dark shape moved along the window and he heard the murmur of another voice, plain in the night: "You got another match, buddy?"

"Yeah, sure," the guard said, as Coppers tried to identify the owner of the first voice. It was familiar to him.

It came to him in a flash, even as he heard the sound of a blow, a muttered, "Ahhhhh," and a sigh.

There was nothing but silence as Coppers waited. The door of the jail rattled and then swung open. Henry Eggert stepped through the door and pulled it shut after him.

Coppers stared at him, trying to pierce the shadows in between, but the light filtering in from outside was uncertain.

"Did you kill that guard?" Coppers asked.

"Hell, no. I hit him with a blackjack I picked up in the deputy's office." Eggert moved to the cell door.

"What the hell do you think you're doing?" Coppers asked angrily.

"Tryin' to get your neck out o' a noose," Eggert said calmly, shoving his hat on the back of his head.

"You got a key to the cell door?"

"No, but I got a couple horseshoe nails. That's all I need for that no-count lock, Coppers."

"Why not call me Butch?" Coppers asked. "Everybody else does."

Busy with his horseshoe nails, Eggert, picking at the lock, said, "I know you ain't Butch. That's one reason I'm here. I don't like to see a man paradin' around under another's name."

"I've never laid claim to that name. What's the other reason you're letting me out?"

"I hate to see a man killed in cold blood, without a chance to defend himself. An' that's what they got lined up for you, ol' buddy."

"And who are 'they'?"

"Farnell. Slim. A real killer name o' Finlay. He killed a man once for starin' at his harelip. That's the three that's aimin' to fix your little red wagon." He muttered a curse, and added: "If you're here when they come, you're a dead man."

"Where did you get all this information?"

Eggert pulled the cell door open and pocketed his horseshoe nails. "I had a meetin'," he said, "with a businessman from Denver. In the hotel. I got there early and while I was waitin' in the hotel room I heard these three talkin' with their boss in the next room."

"Who's the boss?"

"Feller name of Raven."

Raven was Buford Skiles's code name. Coppers' face turned

grim as he realized how Skiles had tricked him. If you couldn't trust your fellow agents, just whom could you trust?

Eggert talked as he moved toward the outside door. "Your buckskin's tied to the deputy's corral gate. There's a bite of grub in your saddlebags. I didn't have time to get much. You'd best be on your way. There's a mob over at the Wild Belle drinkin' up a storm to get to a point where they can swing you." He opened the outside door. "Oh, yeah, I got your gunbelt outta the deputy's office, too, and hung it on your saddle horn."

"Wait a minute," Coppers said.

Eggert paused. "I'm in a mite of a hurry," he said.

"Why are you doing this? Not that I'm not thankful."

"I don't want somebody else takin' my—takin' a name don't belong to 'em. Ain't that good enough?"

"Maybe. You got other reasons?"

"I'd be lyin' out there in that creek with a bullet in my back hadn't been for you," Eggert said. "That counts for somethin'. With me it does."

The door closed on Eggert. By the time Coppers got outside, there was a rapid beat of a hard-running horse, a sound that faded quickly from his hearing.

Buford Skiles reached Arapaho just after dark and rode directly to the hotel. On arriving by train in Laramie he found he'd missed the Arapaho stage. He had no trouble getting a livery-stable horse. He tied his bag to the saddle horn, mounted and headed for Arapaho, driven by an urgency that was new to him.

Now he dismounted in front of the hotel and tied his horse to the rail. He untied his grip and mounted the steps and stood just outside the yellow rectangle of light spilling from the hotel lobby. All activity in the town seemed to center in the two facing saloons down the street. He scowled in the darkness and entered the hotel.

He stood just inside the door, adjusting his eyes to the dim yellow light the oil lamp provided. Outside the island of poor lighting the room was in shadows. He surveyed the warped floors, and sand ground grittily under his boots as he crossed the empty lobby and stood before the counter. He switched the register around and found his name, Raven, scrawled in pencil and the room number. He got the key from the pigeonhole rack behind the counter and mounted the stairs. He unlocked the door and struck a match on the door frame and surveyed the barren interior: an iron bedstead, a washstand with a yellowed pitcher in a chipped bowl, a small cloudy mirror hanging on the wall behind the washstand. A slattern chair stood against the wall. A reflector oil lamp was attached to the wall and he crossed the room, removed the glass globe, and touched his dying match to the wick.

He found himself deliberately suppressing second thoughts he'd been having on this operation. It had all seemed so simple in the beginning, when he'd begun pondering the problem of Coppers, who, he felt, threatened him in some undefinable manner. He remembered how he had struggled with himself in the beginning but finally put all scruples aside and went for it.

There was more to it than his hatred for Coppers. The man, quiet, unassuming but competent, made him feel inferior. Coppers was a better man than he, though he made no visible effort to appear so.

Maybe, Skiles thought, it could have been handled differently. In his larger and original dream he'd not thought of it all ending in a small town where there could be few secrets. Unless he was careful, the rest of the world would learn about him and he couldn't face that thought. Why, he asked himself, had he not taken advantage of that silly weekly shooting match between Coppers and his partner, Gage? It would have been relatively easy to shoot Coppers during one of those fake duels and have Gage take the blame for it. Why? Why? Why?

He muttered a curse and took out his watch and held it to the light. Nearly 10 P.M. and the noise from the saloon seemed to have intensified. He removed his coat and hung it on the back of the rickety chair. He wore a shoulder holster on top of his vest and he didn't bother to remove it. He rolled up his sleeves, noting the grime that had accumulated on his cuffs during the long train ride from Washington, D.C. He washed his hands thoroughly and then his face, drying on the small stiff towel hanging on a nail driven into the washstand. He carefully replaced the towel as a tap sounded on the door.

He went to the door, leaned his head against it, and said cautiously, "Who is it?"

"It's me, Lute Farnell, Mr. Raven."

"And who else?"

"Just me and my men, that's all."

Skiles opened the door and surveyed the three men bulking in the dark hallway. He stepped back from the door and nodded them in. He could smell the rankness of the first man to enter, a slim, almost fragile-appearing man with slumping shoulders and bent knees, who seemed to glide to the bed and to sit upon it in a single motion. Skiles stared fascinated at this man with a thin, skeleton-like face, a harelip which the thin brown scraggly moustache did not conceal.

The other two followed; one sat on the bed beside the harelipped man and the other took the chair. Skiles removed his coat from the chair, shrugging into it.

"These two are Slim Packard and Otis Finlay," Farnell said, gesturing in turn to the two men.

"I thought there were four of you," Skiles said.

"Ah, Mr. Raven, one o' us—that's Dakota—had a accident. His horse stepped in a gopher hole, fell, and pore ol' Dakota got his neck broke."

"Killed him deader'n hell," Slim said solemnly.

Finlay said nothing, staring fixedly at Skiles. That look fostered an uneasiness in Skiles. "You owe me five hundred dollars apiece for five fellers," he said in his strange, nasal intonation. "That's not countin' two sheepherders, an' I'm only chargin' you two-fifty apiece for them account they Meskins."

Skiles stared in fascination at Finlay. "Five men? And two Mexicans—I didn't order any specific—"

"I dunno what specific is," Finlay said. "All I know is I got orders for Gage and Max Callum—and anybody else Coppers talked to more'n say howdy."

"His name is Cassidy," Skiles said. "Butch Cassidy."

"If you say. He was before my time. I kilt seven men and I'm only chargin' you for six. I got Gage at the depot in Cheyenne, and Callum—"

"Don't go into detail," Skiles said hurriedly, taking a wallet from his inside coat pocket. He counted out the bills on top of the washstand while the three of them watched in silence. Skiles gathered the bills and handed them to Finlay.

Finlay wet his thumb and began counting, his lips moving.

"You wanna pay me for Cassidy now?" he asked when he'd finished counting the money.

Skiles's face was pale. The enormity of what he had done, what he planned to do, was beginning to break through the fragile façade he'd raised to rule out other thoughts. He would have bolted out of the room, but he was afraid to move.

"How 'bout the fifty-thousand-dollar reward for Butch Cassidy?" Farnell asked carelessly.

"That'll take some time," Skiles said. "It has to be handled through the deputy. I'm sure he's an honest man and will see that you get the reward."

"Don't make much difference," Farnell said, yawning. He winked at Slim as he spoke and Slim gave a slight nod. "This just about wraps it up, Mr. Raven."

Farnell was standing. Slim and Finlay rose to their feet but didn't move as a great shout went up in the near distance, followed by gunshots. Men were shouting back and forth in hoarse, carrying voices.

"Butch has broke out," Farnell said, and headed for the door. He stopped before he opened the door, whirling, his face twisted in rage. "He'll be headin' for the Slash B," he said tersely. "We'll be waitin' for him when he gets there." He jerked the door open and pounded into the hall.

"I'm going with you," Skiles called. "I must recover that stolen money."

"The hell you say," Farnell said as he plunged down the stairs, followed by Slim and Finlay. He ran on the wooden walk in front of the hotel, and turned in toward the hotel corral. Their horses were tied to the pole fence. The horses shuffled nervously as the three men pounded up to jerk loose the leather lines, mount, and run their horses into the street.

Skiles sat his horse in front of the hotel, waiting. As the three riders ran their horses into the street, Skiles lashed his mount into a gallop, falling in behind them, wondering if he'd be able to keep up with this wild-riding bunch.

Finlay turned in his saddle and fired pointblank into Skiles's body, knocking him from his horse.

Farnell slowed his horse for a moment to allow Finlay to overtake him.

"He ain't gonna recover no nothin'," he said.

CHAPTER TWENTY

Coppers reached the Slash B at that darkest part of the night, just before daybreak. He circled the dark castle, the bunkhouse and barn and corral, keeping Bucky reined to a slow walk. As he rode he kept his ears tuned to the night. He could hear the squeak of the windmill as it turned; he could tell from the frequency of the squeak when the wind freshened or died.

He found nothing unusual in his careful surveillance of the area around the ranch. He stopped once, hearing the thud of hoofs and the squeal of horses at play.

He stopped Bucky near the barn, alert that something had changed, was different. It came to him almost at once that the two large double doors open to the runway of the barn between stalls on both sides were closed. He had never seen them closed before. He got down from his horse and walked to the door and slipped the catch and swung the big doors open.

Three horses stood inside, still saddled and bridled. The horses moved uneasily as he approached them, touched the nearest, finding the hide sweaty and the barrel rising and falling rapidly from making a hard ride. Three riders waited for him inside the castle.

All he must do, he told himself, was to wait them out. Eventually Farnell would come out to make a scout; or send one of his men to do it. At that time he'd make his move, playing his cards as they fell. He tried not to think of Farnell inside the castle, terrorizing Aletha, Wash, and the old man.

He closed and latched the barn door. He circled the castle, judging it was a good two hours until daybreak when there'd be light enough to make out a target for his gun.

Coppers halted beside a young pine tree, smelling the heady odor of needles and cones. A night animal moved off to his right and he automatically catalogued it was a porcupine. His senses already alert became more so; he half-crouched and threw up his arm, as he caught a flash of motion. His reflex action came too late as a blow smashed into his head with a force that toppled him amid a shower of flashing lights. He was unconscious before his body contacted the hard ground.

When he opened his eyes, his head ached. His mind was foggy and he struggled with the puzzling question of why he was lying there in the dirt with a splitting head.

"Got 'im," a nasal voice, nearly unintelligible from a speech defect spoke almost above Coppers.

"Go on, finish him off. Hit him a time er two ag'in." The voice speaking was familiar, but for a half a minute Coppers couldn't remember to whom it belonged. Then it came to him—Slim, Farnell's man.

"Well, I ain't gonna kill him," the first speaker said. "Lute wants him. Let Lute do it if he wants him dead. The money man's dead, Slim, and I don't go 'round killin' people for nothin'."

"Yeah, I know," Slim grunted and grasped Coppers' arm. "Get holt t'other side."

Dragged roughly toward the castle, Coppers remained limp, offering no resistance.

Outside the castle door, Slim yelled, "Light a lamp an' open the damn door."

The door opened and a splash of yellow light fell across Coppers. He closed his eyes.

"If he's gone for, leave him out there," Farnell called. "One dead man in here is one too many."

Who's dead? Coppers wondered. He stopped thinking about it when the two men grabbed him again and dragged him bumping up the steps, across the porch, and into the big front room of the castle.

Coppers, his mind still foggy, had a glimpse of Aletha on the edge of a chair, her shoulders erect and her head up in a proud, defiant way.

Boynton and Washington were missing. One of them must be the dead one, he thought.

Slim and Finlay released Coppers and he dropped, his head thumping against the floor, but he felt nothing.

"He ain't dead," Slim said. "You found out anythin'?"

"I've asked no questions yet," Farnell said and swung around to walk across the room and sit on the edge of the center table. He had his pistol in his hand.

"All right now, Miss Aletha, you want to tell us where all that money is hid?"

Coppers turned his head a fraction and slitted his eyes. Aletha had risen to her feet and was standing near the wall, her head turned toward Coppers. She came haltingly forward, one step, two, and then seemed to orient herself and came steadily and directly to Coppers, kneeling beside him. He felt the softness of her hands as they explored his face, wincing as she touched the open wound where he had been hit. He breathed deeply of her fragrance.

"Washington," she called, "please bring me a pan of water and a washcloth!"

So it was Boynton, Coppers thought, who had died. Had Farnell killed the old man? That'd be another score to settle.

"I ast you a question, missy," Farnell said. "You goin' to answer?"

Coppers' slitted eyes took in the looming black shape of Farnell, with his pistol in his hand. Slim and Finlay stood by the door watching intently.

"He's hurt," Aletha said. "I don't know how bad but he has a head wound." She raised her voice: "Wash, please hurry."

Wash appeared in the doorway bearing a pan. He walked slowly and fearfully by Slim and Finlay and approached Aletha. "Washcloth in the pan, ma'am," he said, and, leaning over, placed the pan on the floor beside Coppers.

Farnell grated, "Damn it, you gonna talk to me?"

"You might just as well settle yourself, Luther Farnell," Aletha said. "I'm going to take care of Dave before I talk to you or anyone."

Farnell erupted with a string of curses, yanking Aletha to her feet, shaking her. "Where's the money?" he yelled. He shook her again.

"The money is gone. Henry Eggert was here and demanded

the money. My grandfather had a heart attack and died. Eggert knew exactly where to find the money. He took it and left."

"Which way did he go?" yelled Farnell, shaking her again.

Coppers, without thinking, launched himself upward, ripping the pistol out of Farnell's hand, and his first shot took out the lamp, leaving the room in darkness. He swung viciously at Farnell with the pistol, feeling the satisfying contact of the metal frame with Farnell's head. At the same time he pulled Aletha to the floor with him as guns thundered in the closed room.

He moved softly, bringing Aletha with him until he was near the entry. He felt Aletha quiver as a gun exploded with a yellow flash and the bullet cracked into the wall. He fired at the yellow flash and his own bullet slapped the wood of the far wall. He moved quickly, taking Aletha with him.

Coppers listened carefully but could hear nothing. He was suddenly aware of the ticking of the clock on the wall.

As he waited, he remembered Harlan Gage smiling at him the last night of his life there in Cheyenne as he wished Coppers well in the venture. He remembered him as he'd first known him and as they grew up together.

Farnell was out cold. He thought his second bullet had taken out Slim. That left the harelipped man, the most dangerous of them all if he was any judge.

Coppers turned cold, feeling the hate wash over him, breaking down all the barriers he'd constructed so carefully since the day McKinley was murdered. He resisted the urge to come up firing blindly. He could wait. Patience hardened him into a rock, as he waited for Finlay to make a sound.

Finlay was patient, too, as the harelipped gunman waited for Coppers to make his own move. Ticking of the clock reminded him that time was running out; how soon before outside light made it possible to shoot? Who would see first. He closed and opened his eyes.

Coppers was suddenly aware of Aletha's hand on his arm. Her fingers slid down his arm to his gun hand. She gripped his hand and raised it, moving it to the right, moving it back and then held it steady. She squeezed his hand and withdrew her hand from his.

He felt the sudden, stepped-up thump of his heart. She had

pinpointed Finlay's position, using her infinitely developed sense of hearing. He sat there so long, his arm frozen in an extended position that he felt an oncoming cramp.

Depressing the trigger of his pistol so there'd be no tattletale clicks, he thumbed back the hammer as far as it would go and allowed it to rest on the full-cock notch.

He hesitated only a moment before touching the trigger lightly, feeling the pistol buck in his hand as flame, smoke, and lead made a savage leap into the darkness. He knew from the sounds—a heavy grunt from Finlay, and the thump of a gun frame on the floor—that Finlay had been hit.

Coppers disengaged himself from Aletha, rising, to feel his way across the room where he lighted a lamp. The heavy smell of coal oil from the shattered lamp hung in the room. He opened the front door and windows and returned to Aletha. He helped her to her feet, hugging her close and leading her to a chair and seating her.

He turned to Farnell who was still unconscious from the blow Coppers had hastily struck a split second after shooting out the lamp.

He went on to Slim, to find the gunman dead, a bullet hole seeping blood just over his right ear. His pistol was cocked and Coppers carefully let the hammer down without removing the gun from Slim's still warm hand. He did not even look at Finlay, nor go near him, feeling a wild, crazy urge to kick the dead man. This was the man who'd killed Harlan Gage, and how many others? He turned back to Aletha.

"I'm sorry about your grandfather," Coppers told Aletha, and then wished he'd said nothing when a tear rolled down one cheek. She dashed it away with a knuckle.

"He had a long and happy life," she said.

"You've got to think of yourself now," Coppers said gently. "Your grandfather would want that. He tried to protect you and to provide for you. That was his greatest goal, Aletha."

She looked at him from teary eyes that tugged at his heart. "Yes, I know, Dave. He talked to me before he—he died. He told me how the money came into his hands. He wasn't a bad man, Dave, simply caught in a trap he didn't devise."

He thought for a moment, feeling uncomfortable with what he

had to say. "I've got to think about getting after Eggert. He has the money and it's my job to get it back."

"I understand, Dave."

"There's things I've got to do," he said awkwardly. "You'll be all right here with Wash. I'll get back soon as I can." He swung through the door, moved down the steps, and across the ground to the barn. Bucky neighed at him, shaking his head impatiently.

"Yeah, yeah," Coppers muttered and offsaddled the buckskin and fed him. He also fed the three horses still standing in the runway of the barn. All the while he mentally went over his moves. He'd hoped to be on Eggert's trail by now. Every-hour country. He was angry that Eggert probably had the money with him when he turned Coppers out of the Arapaho jail.

There were things to be done here before he could ride in pursuit of Eggert. There were two dead men to turn over to Shug Kruger—and one live one, Lute Farnell.

When all the things that had to be done were finished, Coppers halted in mid-stride on his way to the castle. He lifted his eyes to the near ridge to see a group of horsemen surging over the hill. Coppers broke into a run, pounded up the steps and took Aletha by the arm, pushing her toward the door. Once inside he pulled the door shut, turning, drawing his pistol and cocking it.

He made out the bulky shape of Deputy Kruger on the lead horse. Kruger had five men with him and they rode their horses hard into the yard, raising dust as they reined them sharply.

"Put away your gun," Kruger said. "I'm after Farnell and his crew." He took off his hat and bent his head to wipe his forehead on his neckerchief. He replaced his hat, dismounted, and hitched up his pants. "One thing for sure. I know you ain't Butch Cassidy, so you can relax, cowboy, and put that pistol back where it come from."

Coppers holstered his Colt. The door opened behind him and Aletha emerged.

Kruger handed his reins to Pinky. "Why don't you boys water the horses? We'll be headin' out soon's we find out where Farnell is—and his sidekicks."

"Farnell's over there," Coppers said, pointing to the buckboard. "He's alive but Slim Packard and Otis Finlay are not."

Kruger advanced to the porch, a frown of concentration on his ruddy face.

"What's that all about?" he asked.

"I tried to get you to leave a couple of men out here," Coppers said testily, "but you wouldn't do it. Farnell and those two buddies of his broke in the house and tried to get all that booty from Mr. Boynton."

"And if it hadn't been for Dave they might have got it," Aletha said.

"Ah, I don't think so," Kruger said smugly. "That money is being held in the bank vaults in Arapaho and will be sent to wherever the Treasury man says to send it." His chest swelled and it was plain he was pleased with himself.

"There's more to it than that," Coppers said.

"Sure's hell. When you broke out o' jail, we took out after you —or thought we did. Turned out it wasn't you a tall but ol' Henry Eggert. Henry had a big bunch o' money with him. An' another feller, name of Lem Taylor, was also carryin' a hell of a lot o' money."

"Between the two of them, a little less than two million dollars," Coppers said.

"Don't say! Well, we took Eggert and Taylor back to Arapaho and put 'em both in jail." He put a finger to his nose and scratched.

"I hope you didn't leave any horseshoe nails in Eggert's pocket," Coppers said.

"Horseshoe nails? Most riders carry a few."

"But not all of them use the nails the way Eggert does. He opened the lock on your jail with two horseshoe nails."

"The hell you say!"

Coppers nodded. "He let me out of jail."

"Well, I'll be damned. He's one who hit Pinky? That Pinky got a knot on his head the size a goose aig." His face brightened. "Here's sumpin betcha don't know: We found a man near dead in the street close t' the hotel. Name o' Skiles; seems he's a Secret Service feller just like you, Coppers. An' he was up to his eyebrows in a scheme that's purt far-fetched. Seems Skiles hatched up a plan to bring Butch Cassidy back and then capture him, dead o' course, an' that's how he hired Farnell and his buddies to watch for you and turn you in just at the right time. Trouble is, somehow Farnell found out about the money an' started tryin' to get his hands on it. Lot o' men died because of that money, Coppers. Finlay killed six or seven and Skiles paid him for it."

"Dakota was used as a messenger to carry the money into Arapaho for mailing to Taylor," Coppers said thoughtfully. "I believe Farnell or Slim killed Dakota when they found out about it. But, back to Skiles. He told you he paid Finlay to kill?"

Kruger shook his head. "Nope. He told it to the doctor in Arapaho who took care o' him—or tried to. Skiles didn't have a chance. Farnell or one of his crew, probably Finlay, shot him at close range. Didn't live long but before he died told Doc Parks all about it. Doc wrote it down. Deathbed confession, you might say."

The posse straggled back from watering the horses and stood by silently.

"Gotta get ridin'," Kruger said. "You got me worried, Coppers, tellin' me Henry Eggert can open my jail with a horseshoe nail."

"He uses two nails," Coppers said.

Kruger slapped his thigh. "Let's move it out, boys."

"Wait," Coppers said. "Did Taylor do any talking?"

"Did he? Never quit. He was still talkin' when I locked the door on him. Seems he had a deal with ol' man—Mr. Boynton that is—to spread the money around. But Taylor got hungry, wanted it all 't once. Hired Henry Eggert and Spud Oliver to come up and take it all. Henry took so long that Taylor got worried and come up to Arapaho to speed things up. He got here just in time to ride off with Eggert. But we caught 'em, by damn!"

Kruger turned, barking orders, and then led Coppers aside. "I got nothin' again you personal. You had a job to do and done it best you could. But there's lots o' hard feelin's about you from people around here."

"That's their lookout," Coppers said.

"Well, maybe. I jes' wanted you to know. Mammas scare their kids to bein' good by tellin' 'em Coppers gonna get 'em."

Coppers made an impatient motion. "I'm ready to fade out of here. I'd like for you to escort Aletha to Arapaho so she can get the stage to Laramie and catch an eastbound."

"Whatever fur?"

"She's all alone now. There's an operation that may restore her sight. I'm advising her to go back and have it done."

Kruger squinted at him. "Are you, now? Well, that young lady thinks a heap o' you, Coppers. She might have second thoughts if she could see. Get what I mean?"

"My question was, will you escort her to Arapaho?"

"Oh, sure. I'm wearin' this star to serve all the law-abidin' citizens in the county." He wheeled and went toward the buckboard where Farnell sat, his wrists tied together and his feet roped to a wagon-seat spring. Finlay's and Slim's bodies, wrapped in canvas, occupied the back part of the buckboard.

"Farnell, you remember the first night I got here?" Coppers asked.

Farnell didn't raise his head and didn't answer.

"That night there was a lot of shooting up the canyon," Coppers went on. "You want to tell me about that?"

"Go to hell," Farnell said.

"You won't git nothin' outta him," Kruger said.

Aletha came down the steps of the castle and Coppers went to meet her. She heard his footsteps, halted, waiting. He came close to her and she moved beside him, slipping her hand between his side and his arm. "Now that everything is settled," she said, "you won't have to leave to go after Henry Eggert. He's safely in jail."

"There's one other," Coppers said uncomfortably.

"Oh, no," she said.

"Yes. A man named Gard. Buel Gard. He was with the bunch that kidnaped you. He's the one sent to carry a ransom note to your grandfather, but I intercepted him and took the note. I warned him to leave the country but he might still be around. I'll make a search and make sure he's gone from this part of the country."

"You've done your job," declared Aletha. "More than that, even. I get a dreadful feeling that if Eggert and Gard were both safely under lock and key, you'd find someone else to look for."

He felt a shock at her words. Had he really got caught up into the manhunting business to the exclusion of all else? He was aware that it could happen to a man. He forced a laugh. "No,

That can't happen to me. The most important thing right now is you, what's to be done about your—your eyesight."

"I thought I'd remain here for the time being."

"That's almost impossible," he said reluctantly. "Your grandfather wanted your sight restored more than he wanted anything else in the world. You owe it to him—and to yourself—to do this, Aletha."

She turned her head. "What about you? How do you feel about it?"

"I want you to do it," he said.

She dropped her hand from his arm. "You're right, of course," she said. "It'll take me at least a week to get ready."

"I asked Deputy Kruger to escort you to Arapaho today," Coppers said. "You can take the stage from there to Laramie and catch the eastbound train."

She spoke in a subdued voice. "If that's what you want."

CHAPTER TWENTY-ONE

Except for an aching void at Aletha's absence, the passing summer proved uneventful. He wakened one morning to find white frost covering the countryside. A thin skim of ice appeared on the watering troughs, and the higher country was aflame with the brilliant reds of the brush oak and the soft gold of quaking aspen. The horses breathed steam as they clustered near the fence waiting to be fed.

He'd finished the chores and was washing up for breakfast when he heard a hail from outside. He stepped through the back door and went to the ground, sliding toward the front of the house, his hand on his gun.

He relaxed when he saw Bennion fighting a team of matched blacks. Bennion got them under control as Coppers approached the surrey. Sal sat in the back seat with the little girl on one side of her and Tommie on the other, all of them covered by a lap robe.

"Hi ya, Dave," Bennion hailed.

Coppers reached the surrey, leaned forward and chucked the little girl under the chin, and then tipped Tommie's hat over his eyes. The two kids, giggling, disappeared under the lap robe.

"You're out early," he said to Bennion.

"Come by to see if you'd go to Laramie with us," he said. "Sheriff's office called and said they're holdin' Farnell's hearing and need you to testify."

"Sure, I'll ride in," Coppers said.

"Tie your horse in back and ride up here," Bennion said. "I want t' talk to you."

"Sure. I'll get ready." He held out his hand to Sal. "Come on in the house and have some coffee while you wait. I think Wash can find something for the kids."

Tommie and the little girl heard and popped out from under the lap robe, their eyes shining with excitement. "What's Wash got for us?" Tommie wanted to know.

"He'll find something," Coppers promised and helped Sal to the ground and then lifted the children from the surrey.

Coppers ate his breakfast while Sal and Mel drank coffee and the children munched on doughnuts as only Washington could make them.

"Have you heard from Aletha?" Sal asked shyly.

"I got a telegram she'd got there safely. Nothing since."

"That hearin' might be big news," Bennion offered, "but it ain't the biggest by far. President Roosevelt's comin' to Laramie, on his way to Yellowstone to hunt bear an' elk. He's makin' a speech durin' the stop in Laramie, and the town is sure puttin' out the welcome mat for him."

When Coppers came out of the castle, the Bennions had already loaded into the surrey. Bennion looked at Coppers in surprise. Ida Mae had mailed his brown corduroy suit and he was dressed in his normal Washington attire.

"By golly, Dave, you look like you just stepped outta the Cheyenne Social Club," Bennion declared.

Coppers tied Bucky to the endgate of the surrey, climbed beside Bennion, and the two blacks took off.

Bennion let them run for a while before pulling them in. He obviously had something on his mind and he finally got to it.

"You know how I hate to mess around the dudes," he said. "It's not that they're not good people, maybe spoiled some, and kind of ignorant, but I can't abide 'em. I need a good trail boss to take charge. Those trips up in the mountain are what they all like and I want to keep them goin'. But I can't stand the thought of doin' it myself. What I'm gettin' at is this—you take charge of that end of it and I'll do the rest. You're the man for the job, Dave. You got a kind of air that makes people look to you for guidance. I'm willin' to make you part owner if you'll go in with me."

Coppers said nothing for a long period while the surrey creaked over the road at a good pace. Then he said, "I appreciate your offer, Mel. I can't do it for a lot of reasons."

"Think about it," Bennion urged. "I'll make up a financial statement so you can see for yourself how it stands."

"I don't know what I'll be doing," Coppers said. "But I do know I can't throw in with you. Anyway, Mel, you've got a good man or two out there who'd fit in just fine. Grady'd make a good trail boss for your dudes."

Bennion was silent for the remainder of the ride to Laramie. The town was dressed for the presidential visit. Bunting flew in the brisk wind. The fireman's band tuned up on a platform that had been erected near the railroad siding where the Presidential Special would be spotted. Laramie citizens turned out en masse in their Sunday finery.

Bennion put Sal and the children off at the hotel and then drove on to the livery stable to care for the horses. His friends from out in the county stopped him and talked to him while pointedly ignoring Coppers.

After the animals were cared for, Bennion said, "Let's have just one," and led the way to the nearest saloon. They found the place crowded but edged into a space at the end of the bar and silently toasted one another.

The bar talk was all of Roosevelt's impending visit. There was vibrant excitement in the air as men pushed in and out of the saloons or clustered in knots on the street.

A railroad callboy stuck his head between the batwing doors and shouted, "Special's 'bout twenty minutes out!"

There began a slow exodus from the saloon as Coppers and Bennion finished their drinks. They walked out of the saloon into the bright sunshine and into the crowd. People filled the wooden walk with the overflow spilling out into the street. Small boys raced up and down the street and through the alleys. Occasionally a firecracker exploded. A huge sign had been erected over the bandstand which read in large black letters: WELCOME PRES. ROOSEVELT TO TEDDY COUNTRY.

"By God, it's bigger'n I thought it'd be," Bennion said, pleased. "You see what's gonna happen, Dave?"

"I don't see," Coppers confessed.

"We got a man for President who thinks like us. He's made the whole damn country know all about us. That means more business for us. He's good for business."

"Good for the dude business?"

"All business," Bennion declared expansively. "Just as soon as the county fixes the road between here and the Box MB, I'm gonna buy one a them gas buggies to haul the pilgrims out t' the ranch."

"The stagecoach is a big attraction, Mel."

"Yeah, well, I guess. But it's a pain in the backsides. I'm gonna give the damn stage to the school district if they promise not to sell it off. I want the kids in the future to see what we had to ride in. Wasn't for the bad roads, I'd buy a gas buggy right now. But I'm not about to ask the commissioners to fix the roads. When the county got its charter they made a vow to hang, drown, or run outta the country anybody asking for improvements that cost money. Hey, here she comes!"

Bennion followed Coppers as he half ran toward the depot as the train groaned to a halt, its whistle blowing, the bell ringing, and clouds of steam billowing out.

Roosevelt emerged from the end car to the platform, his arms raised above his head, smiling and nodding as the crowd roared a welcome.

Coppers, standing in the back fringes of the crowd, was aware again of the man's charisma. Doesn't look any older than the day we disbanded on Long Island, he thought. He'd found the colonel to be a man who generated deep feelings. He'd never lost his respect and affection for Roosevelt.

The people fell silent as Roosevelt began to speak in his characteristically vigorous manner.

"Thank you for that welcome," he said. "I always feel at home here. I was born in the East but I'm a Westerner.

"This is a country that has entered into the very marrow of my being. I come here as often as I can for a renewal of spirit. Yes, and to try to see things through your eyes. That's my reality.

"Let me tell you that I first came to the West with as good an education as money can buy. I was knowledgeable in the world of books but it was in this vast, marvelous country that I learned about men. I owe more than I can express to the West, our West. I would that all of America be infused with that spirit of the West.

"Had I not come to know the West in my youth, I may never

have become your President. I know that you Westerners are the kind of men to have along when trouble comes.

"One of the men who went to Cuba with me is among you today." He straightened, squaring his shoulders, adjusting his glasses, looking out over the crowd. "Is Dave Coppers out there?"

"Go on up!" Bennion shouted, giving Dave a push. The crowd parted and rough hands shoved Coppers forward. He went unwillingly, pushed along by men who in the not distant past had looked the other way when he walked the streets.

President Roosevelt leaned down, shook hands with Coppers and, retaining his hand, pulled him up to the platform. Beyond, through the door, Coppers could see Chief Effington standing inside the Pullman car.

Roosevelt was speaking again: "I'll always be in Coppers' debt. He saved my life. He saved one of my horses. He's as good a man as I ever rode with. And now we've got things to talk about."

Roosevelt and Coppers entered the Pullman car with the crowd roaring approval, tentatively at first, then expanding into a sustained ovation that penetrated inside the car even with the door closed.

In the small anteroom just inside the door, Chief Effington stood stiffly at attention as Coppers and Roosevelt entered. "Chief Effington is retiring soon," Roosevelt said. "I want you for his replacement, Sergeant. Wait, now, don't answer me at this moment." He gave Coppers a gentle push toward the interior of the private car. "Go on in there for a surprise. Chief Effington and I will join you later."

Coppers surveyed the gleaming interior of the presidential car, the highly polished ceiling, crystal chandeliers and luxurious cushioned chairs and couches. The carpeted, thick-piled floor gave no sound as he walked forward. Someone was seated in one of the backward-facing leather-covered chairs.

Aletha rose, turned and, smiling, said, "Dave!" in a warm and happy voice.

He stood there, transfixed, and then she came to him. He put out his hands and pulled her close, his heartbeat stepping up as he saw her lips tremble a little. A great flame roared up when he kissed her and again he felt the rush of feelings he'd not considered possible. Her hands touched his face and he remembered their coolness, and he remembered the odor of flowers, her fragrance.

"Aletha," he said. "You can see?"

"Yes. Oh, yes and yes and yes!"

He drew back. "Then—then, now that you can see me, maybe—"

Her fingers touched his face again, moved lightly over his hair, his eyes, and lips; and then her arms, strong, pulled his head down. "You look exactly as I pictured you would look," she said softly.

The door opened behind them but neither of them were aware that the President of the United States had peered in and, though he loved to be the center of attention, softly withdrew, telling his aides, "We'll enter the other way." He paused on the step. "By George, this has been a bully, bully day!"